YESHUA'S THIEF

If you've ever wondered what it was like to live "back in the day" when Jesus walked among us, this novel takes you there with compelling characters and a rich setting that come alive through a moving story that weaves imagination and Bible history together to make it relatable and real.

—**Michele Chynoweth,** bestselling author of *The Jealous Son, The Runaway Prophet, The Peace Maker,* and *The Faithful One*

R.E. Addison has written a gripping, compelling, and very moving novel, expanding an obscure character from the word of God. You will be drawn in immediately as you go on a revealing and challenging journey with *Yeshua's Thief!*

—**Greg and Julie Gorman,** authors, speakers, and founders of Married for A Purpose.

R.E. Addison takes his readers on a suspenseful journey with twists and turns that ultimately remind us all that the grace of God can truly forgive your past, empower your present, and secure your future. I can hardly wait for the sequel.

—**Stan Coleman,** pastor and church consultant, Marietta, Georgia

Growing up without a dad was hard and painful, but knowing my dad lived an honorable life of integrity made it bearable. He died when I was two at the hands of a drunk driver. Hearing the anguish of a son who hated a father who chose a life of crime over a loving family brought this favorite and most powerful demonstration of redemption and mercy to life for me. *Yeshua's Thief* is real and raw as the son of a thief grapples with living with an unwanted legacy that threatens to leave his own life in ruins. This book offers a firsthand look at pain, grief, and rejection but with the hope of forgiveness and unconditional love. It is my honor to highly recommend *Yeshua's Thief* as a book you must read.

—**Janan Olsen,** educator, serving as a university instructor and middle and high school public school teacher

For many of us, the characters in the Bible seem as flat as the flannelboard pictures of them we played within Sunday School. *Yeshua's Thief* brings several of these characters off the page and into life. The reader is pulled into a world of love, cruelty, fortune, lies, and redemption. You will never think of the thief on the cross in the same way after reading this book!

—**Diane Castro**, owner of Sweet Home Books, Wetumpka Alabama.

YESHUA'S THIEF

A NOVEL

R.E. ADDISON

NEW YORK

LONDON • NASHVILLE • MELBOURNE • VANCOUVER

YESHUA'S THIEF
A NOVEL

Published in New York, New York, by Morgan James Publishing. Morgan James is a trademark of Morgan James, LLC. www.MorganJamesPublishing.com

Morgan James BOGO™

A **FREE** ebook edition is available for you or a friend with the purchase of this print book.

CLEARLY SIGN YOUR NAME ABOVE

Instructions to claim your free ebook edition:
1. Visit MorganJamesBOGO.com
2. Sign your name CLEARLY in the space above
3. Complete the form and submit a photo of this entire page
4. You or your friend can download the ebook to your preferred device

ISBN 978-1-63195-531-0 paperback
ISBN 978-1-63195-532-7 ebook
Library of Congress Control Number:
2021902347

Cover Design by:
Rachel Lopez
www.r2cdesign.com

Morgan James is a proud partner of Habitat for Humanity Peninsula and Greater Williamsburg. Partners in building since 2006.

Get involved today! Visit
MorganJamesPublishing.com/giving-back

For my grandmother Marilyn (Mee-Maw) Addison.
Your constant prayers and dedication to your family will be
felt for many generations. Our family will indeed
be an unbroken circle in heaven.

ACKNOWLEDGMENTS

There are always so many people to thank when it comes to any creative work. The best works require a team, and *Yeshua's Thief* is no different. First, I would like to thank my Lord and Savior Jesus Christ, who made the kind of forgiveness this book illustrates possible through his willing sacrifice on the Cross. Next, I would like to thank my wife, Blanca, for encouraging me to finish the works I have started. I love you more than you can ever know. I would also like to thank my two children, Ryan and Karlie, for putting up with a dopey dad who likes to run these story ideas by them. A special thanks to my parents, Rick and Karon, who took in this foster kid and gave him a forever home, instilling God's love and values which I hope to pass down to my children as well.

Many thanks to my editorial team, Angie and Emily Kiesling, and the people at Editorial Attic for seeing the potential in this story and for the constant revisions that made it the story it is today. Thanks to Cortney Donelson and the team at vocem, LLC for the final pairs of eyes to make the book ready for publishing.

To Greg and Julie Gorman, who, upon hearing the idea for this novel, connected me with Terry Whalen and the Morgan James

Publishing team. To the team at Morgan James Publishing for giving this story a chance.

I want to thank everyone involved in the drama team at The Grace Place and made the story of *Yeshua's Thief* come alive.

And finally, I want to thank you, dear reader, for reading this story in its entirety and opening your heart to reading the writings of a flawed and grateful writer.

PREFACE

I believe it is important to note that Biblical text does not say much about the thief on the Cross. The little we know about the thief lends itself to the belief that he still had a glimmer of humanity left in his soul. The Bible is not clear about his motivations, station in life, or how he knew of Yeshua. It just includes a conversation as he was dying. The following story is a work of fiction, and I wrote it because I believe there must be more to this man than just one significant moment in history. He must have had a family. The chances are good that the family would have been considered a broken one. We do not know if he had any children or a wife.

We can surmise, however, that he knew in part some of the teachings of Yeshua. He knew enough to confess his guilt. He knew that Yeshua was the Son of God. He also knew that he needed mercy, not for this life, but for eternity as well. The story of the thief, though sad, is hopeful for many of us. The forgiveness offered him has given hope to countless people who have made mistakes and have come to know the life-saving Grace and Mercy of God the Father through the Son.

I pray this story will remind you of your journey and the times when forgiveness was difficult to find.

The story of Yeshua's Thief is, in many ways, all our stories. We all deserve the thief's sentence. We all need forgiveness. And, even if you are not a believer, I hope you can find enjoyment and hope within these pages.

PROLOGUE

"My boy should be about fifteen now," said Dismas while pulling his sword. Using a small smooth stone and some olive oil, he honed the edge.

"Why do you bring that up now?" asked Rasheed.

"No reason." Dismas peered over the rock outcropping.

"You said they were coming this way today. Right?"

"Yes. It was in an invitation for Pilate himself."

Rasheed stood up to get a better view.

Secretly Dismas hoped for a reprieve from the fighting and the pillaging. He was down to two men, and one of those, he was sure, was not coming back from visiting his family in Nazareth. They had been dealt a crushing blow by the Romans. He still smelled of smoke from the fire.

"Rasheed, I know you want revenge for last night, but we're exhausted. It might be wise to blend in and get some rest before we go

1

sabotaging the shipment against men who have a lot of training and are very rested compared to us."

"If we do that, then we lose the element of surprise," said Rasheed. "Besides, what are we going to go back to if we don't succeed?"

"That's precisely it. They don't know who we are yet. Our families are safe for now."

"Your family is safe. Mine are all dead."

"You see, I knew that, and . . ." said Dismas.

"It's alright. It's been a few years. But if we don't do this, they died for nothing."

Dismas noticed Rasheed's mouth quiver.

"Well, it looks like you're going to get your wish. Look!" Dismas pointed at the wagon pulled by four horses.

"They're moving fast for this pass. This only works to our advantage. Get in position."

Rasheed took his orders and ran through the maze of boulders to the edge of the pass. Leaning down into the dirt, he picked up the end of the rope they had laid out and buried across the path the night before. The rope was woven with sharp bone and metal bits to make sure the horses sustained damage, making retreat next to impossible.

The sound of roaring hooves was within earshot, though the sound was not clear yet.

Dismas ran to his position just three hundred paces ahead of the trail and climbed to the top of a large boulder. He picked up the bow and arrows he positioned there the night before. The sound of the roaring hooves slowly increased in volume. The detail only consisted of four Roman soldiers plus a driver. They were riding on either side of the carriage keeping a steady pace. Dismas knew they had to kill all the soldiers, or they would be found out quickly and executed.

He could see Rasheed from his perch. Slowly, Dismas drew his bowstring. Misjudging the distance, Dismas held it there for what seemed like forever. He could feel his arms quivering, and his muscles began to fatigue. "Steady," he told himself. He didn't release the arrow until all he could see was his first target. The arrow released through sheer exhaustion.

Silently the projectile flew through the air, hitting below his mark. He could see the horse's front legs give way underneath the soldier, sending its rider flying forward and onto the rope. The carriage tried to stop, but it was too late. Rasheed pulled hard on the rope, wrapping the other end around the tree. The rope did not have its intended effect. The weight of the soldier held it down, and the carriage ran over him and the rope.

Dismas nocked another arrow and sent it in the direction of the driver. This time it found its mark, pinning the driver to the wooden seat. Now the cart banked hard to the right, careening on its side and strewing its contents all over the desert floor. The other three soldiers found cover behind several rocks. Dismas scanned the area for a hint at where they might be hiding. He caught a glare off one of their helmets. Nocking another arrow, he quickly aimed and sent it flying. The arrow glanced off the rocks and found the leg of the soldier. He noticed Rasheed running through the maze of rocks. He was so mesmerized by his comrade's ability that he failed to see the other two soldiers making their way to his perch. Shaking off his trance, Dismas looked around for the other two. He couldn't see them. Turning in a circle, he scanned the rest of the countryside. Then he heard one of the men slip on the loose rocks to his left. His initial reaction was to send an arrow in that direction. However, when he reached for his quiver, there were none left.

Drawing his sword, he slid off his perch, landing on the parched earth. Seemingly from out of nowhere, Rasheed charged the Roman, looping the rope around the Roman's neck and pulling with all his might. The metal shards dug deep into the guard's jugular, staining the rope and his white tunic red. Putting his foot on the Roman's chest to keep his leverage, he pushed the man down to the ground until he saw no movement.

As Dismas slowly approached, an arrow sailed past his ear and lodged itself into Rasheed's stomach. Ducking down and turning in one swift motion, Dismas caught the other guard, who was charging him with a spear.

His sword caught the man at the base of the chin, severing blood vessels and the bones at the base of his skull.

The Roman shuddered as he crumpled to the ground in a bloody mess next to the bow Dismas had dropped on his way down from the boulder. Standing up, Dismas ran to Rasheed's side only to hear him gasp for breath one last time—his eyes permanently open in shock.

Dismas bowed his head in respect. With two fingers, he shut the eyelids of his friend and prayed.

Now, it was just Dismas.

With no men left to lead and no one to help him bury the dead, he slowly walked over to the cargo thrown out of the carriage. A glint of something shiny caught his eye. He walked over to see a wooden box. Gilded in fine silver, it had an inscription engraved into the metal lid.

"A gift for one of the most gifted leaders of whom I entrusted the Judean territory. May this token of appreciation for your loyalty and service to Tiberius Caesar Augustus serve you and your household well."

When he opened the lid, he couldn't believe what he saw—a dagger. The finest craftmanship Dismas had ever seen. The most valuable object he had ever held in his hands. And now it was his. *I can't keep the box,* he thought. He knew the inscription would give away the fact that the dagger was stolen. Ripping out the box's lining, he wrapped the blade and stuffed it into his satchel.

Just up the road, he could hear the clod of hooves beating the compact earth. He had to move quickly. Running into the brush, he ducked down to his stomach so he could see under the brush.

A Roman cart with a family pulled up. An apparent husband and wife stopped to survey the damage. With them were two teenagers.

"Asher!" called the man.

The teenage boy stood to attention.

"Look for the dagger. I fear it has been stolen."

The teenage boy stepped down from the wagon and began looking through the wreckage. Dismas could see the boy picking up the empty box.

"Abigail! Help your brother!"

"Aw, dad. Do I have to?"

"I said to get down there!"

The father barked as he pushed her off the cart. The daughter fell to the ground. Dismas could see her pocket some of the strewn coins when her father was distracted.

The bodies were fresh, and Dismas knew the father sensed his presence. Each of the teenagers filled a bag with as many coins as they could carry. The father scanned the horizon looking for God knew what. The girl was close enough for Dismas to see her bruised face. He tightened his grip on his sword.

"Alright, get back up here," called the man. "We'll never make Tiberias if we sit here looking for the gift. It was most likely stolen." Asher and Abigail did as they were told.

"We have to hurry. Your new husband awaits," he said to Abigail.

"I could never love him. He's disgusting!"

The father backhanded his daughter, the sound of his hand so loud that Dismas expected her to spit some of her teeth out.

Why would a father do that to such a beautiful girl? He waited for the cart to start moving again. When they passed him, he ran back, pulled an arrow from the body of his friend. Climbing to the boulder's top where he was initially perched, he nocked the arrow. *God? May this arrow find its mark and free this young lady,* he prayed. The arrow released with a hiss. Time slowed down as Dismas watched the arrow hit its mark, right through the man's neck. He could see that Abigail spotted him. The wife wailed out loud as the man slumped over. Dismas ducked down.

Asher took the reins and, with a yell, pushed the horses to a gallop, making their escape. The body of the man fell off the cart and landed with a sickening, lifeless thud.

Dismas collapsed in exhaustion. He knew he had to get up, but every muscle in his body ached. Slowly, he walked in the opposite direction.

The dagger tucked into his waist was still covered by the cloth. There was no way to sell this thing soon. By now, the Romans would have everyone in Judea looking for this treasure. The desert sun beat down on his head. He had lost his head covering in the exchange.

Dripping with sweat, he pushed on until he could see the outskirts of the city. He knew it was a risk coming to Tiberias, but his family was here. He could make camp by the Sea of Galilee and clean up. Walking forward, his legs trembled. He was fortunate enough to make it to the sea. He jumped in for a swim, gulping down mouthfuls of the life-giving liquid.

The sea was more a freshwater lake than a sea. The cool water dulled the bloodstains in his garments to a light brown. When darkness came, he made a fire. His clothes were almost dry now, and he felt refreshed. He had money to buy food when he felt it was safe to go into the city. Aaliyah, his wife, would not be happy to see him. She disapproved of his political leanings and activist ways. His son, whom he'd not seen in years, must look quite grown up now. A tear formed in the corner of his eye as the fire absorbed his emotions in the quiet crackling. The flames licking over his firewood were hypnotic, and he soon fell asleep.

CHAPTER 1

As morning dawned on the city, Ezekiel walked home from the market with a basket of fresh fish. The scent of freshly baked bread rose to his nostrils through clean air. His father had given him a thin copper coin to buy the family's daily food. The pit of his stomach churned as if a spirit was trying to make butter in his belly. It was the same churning as when he once got lost in the hills.

He didn't feel right buying food with Roman money, which was out of his father's character. Dismas, his father, hated the Romans. Even though he was careful, the hatred bubbled to the surface when he had too much wine. It always upset Aaliyah, Ezekiel's mother, who sent him to the market to talk privately with Dismas.

Ezekiel inhaled deeply and could almost taste the musht. It had been some time since they had such a treat. Ezekiel carried a sense of expectation along with the basket as he made his way up the hillside to his clay house. Across the street stood his grandfather, Elyam.

"Hi, Ezekiel. Your grandmother sent me out here to ask you to gather some firewood. If you would like, I could help you."

Ezekiel smiled. "Anything for my favorite grandfather."

"I wasn't aware of you having another grandfather somewhere."

"Exactly my point." Ezekiel smiled. He admired Elyam for his steadiness. Unlike his father, Elyam was well respected by his family and friends.

On the other hand, Dismas did not share the values of the rest of the family. Still, he loved Aaliyah with unending passion. He continually sought to win over her affection with lavish gifts. The day before, the gift had been a sack of Roman copper coins.

Ezekiel wanted to believe his father's exotic tales of adventure that he occasionally spun to account for the seemingly miraculous gifts. Still, they seemed too fantastic to be true.

As he neared the door, Aaliyah burst onto the street, her eyes telling the story of her heart as they often did. With one look, Ezekiel suspected this would be the last time, for a long time, that he would lay eyes on his father. Walking through the open door, he could sense the familiar tension and said nothing as he laid down the fish in the small alcove beside the clay oven.

Dismas sat on his haunches in the corner with the tail of his cloak piling in the dirt. He dragged his finger on the ground in circular patterns as if contemplating what to say next. Ezekiel went up to him and hugged him with intensity.

Dismas put his arm around his son and slowly stood up. Then he turned.

"I have a gift for you."

"Really? What is it?" Ezekiel looked at his father, not knowing if he could trust him. Dismas returned the look with a discerning impression as if to signal that this gift was great and came with responsibility. Then, suddenly, he pulled out a sheathed dagger. The crafting was more beautiful than anything Ezekiel had seen before, with a gold inlay and a pearl-studded hilt. Again, Ezekiel's heart sank into his stomach.

"It's really more of a loan. Keep it safe until I return."

"Why are you giving it to me?"

"Because, Ezekiel, I believe I can trust you. Am I right?"

"Of course."

"Good. I am going away for a while. Please keep it safe. Bury it if you must. Whatever you do, do not lose it."

"When will you return?"

"I don't know. Maybe a few months. Maybe never."

Ezekiel promptly hid the dagger amidst his cloaks. He didn't like hiding things. It made him feel like a cheat. However, he was a good son and did as he was told. He planned to steal off in the night and bury it under the olive tree that Elyam planted when he was born. For the moment, all he could do was tell his father goodbye.

The weight of the moment caught the young boy like a swift punch to the stomach. So he ran out of the house along the path by the sea. People didn't seem to notice, and if they saw him, they didn't seem to care.

It was a harsh time to be a boy of fifteen in Galilee. He was old enough to carry responsibilities but young enough to carry a hopeful heart within him everywhere. Unfortunately, being hopeful sometimes felt like carrying a cup around that other people would fill with a bitter drink. He slumped against the wall, skidding to the floor, and let his tears flow.

He was so overcome with emotion that he failed to see the approaching Roman soldier. Most of the time, he could avoid such annoyances, but with his head down, he was unable to move out of the way before it was too late.

"You, there!" said the soldier. The sun glistened off his armor like shimmering water.

Ezekiel slowly looked up to see the face of the oppressor. "Yes, I said you! Carry my shield, for I am tired and in need of rest."

"Yes, sir." Ezekiel wiped his cheeks on the short sleeves of his tunic, fearing the consequences of a response that could be taken as impertinent. He stood and picked up the shield, which was so heavy that he had to sling it onto his back, causing him to stumble. This brought a peal of laughter from the soldier.

Sweat poured over Ezekiel's forehead as he struggled to keep up with the soldier. His muscles ached, and his side felt the sharp pain of a cramp as he neared the obligatory mile required under Roman law. Ezekiel knew the measurement of a mile was a relative distance. It was almost always exaggerated to mean as far as the soldier needed to go.

Looking past the guard, he saw his friend Rina with a basket of grain under her arm. Even under the weight of the shield, he took notice of how much she had changed over the last few years. Every day, it seemed, she grew visibly in her womanhood.

Rina looked at him and nodded. Ezekiel knew then that his mother would soon understand why he would be coming home late.

"Keep your eyes focused on the path. I have an important meeting tonight and need to get there quickly." The flat side of the Roman's sword came crashing down on Ezekiel's left shoulder, causing him to stumble. Again, a cruel laugh came from the Roman, who then swiftly kicked him in the stomach, sending Ezekiel sprawling to the ground.

Rina came running to him and tried to help him up, which prompted the soldier to grab her by the hair and throw her to the side.

He picked up the shield, cursed under his breath, and walked away, leaving Rina and Ezekiel lying together, face-down in the street.

"Are you alright?" Ezekiel asked Rina, struggling to get up.

No answer came, only sobbing. Ezekiel realized Rina had hit her head on a stone.

"Rina?" Still, she laid there sobbing. Ezekiel forced himself to his feet. Once he was up, he felt a little better. He took a few steps over to Rina, who tried on her own to get up. Grabbing her arm, he helped her to her feet, which seemed to give her strength. He bandaged her forehead with strips torn from his tunic, and they hobbled home arm-in-arm.

The arid climate of Tiberias seemed to choke the life out of Ezekiel. His mother came rushing out to meet them. Ezekiel could see that tears streaked down her cheeks as she grabbed him and held his head close to her heart.

Rina stumbled to her knees. Aaliyah caught her by the arm then knelt to face her, wrapping her in a tight embrace.

Rina continued to cry. Ezekiel noticed her resolve didn't falter even when her body did. It made her even more attractive.

"Let's go inside," said Aaliyah. "Come, Rina, we'll find a place for you to lie down." Rina just nodded. Ezekiel was glad she was there, though he would have spared her this pain if he could. He could tell Rina was forcing a smile as Aaliyah helped her inside. Out of respect, Ezekiel sat outside on the west side of the house and watched the sun fade from view behind the roofs of Galilee. Aaliyah brought Ezekiel some fish and bread, along with some water in a clay pot. The cold liquid felt kind to his throat, and the salty fish tasted like a little bit of heaven, given how tired he was. When the sun was nearly hidden from view, Rina's mother, Ester, came home from working the vineyards.

"Thank you for protecting Rina, Ezekiel," she said as she reemerged from the house with Rina under her wing. Ezekiel smiled as they walked away. His heart lightened at the thought that his best friend was going to be alright.

"I'll come by to check on you tomorrow."

Rina just forced a smile. "It's been a long day," said Ester.

CHAPTER 2

F our years passed since Dismas's disappearance.

Ezekiel found work at the fish market, buying and selling the day's catch from Galilee. It was a demanding job, and Ezekiel had to work harder than most to earn enough. Even so, Ezekiel found it fulfilling to be productive and provide for his mother and grandparents. After all, there weren't many occupations left for a Jewish boy with no father to pass a trade down to him. He was not a Levite, so he could not go into the priesthood. He owned very little property, so farming was out of the question. He could, however, save enough money to buy a boat of his own someday. For now, he could sell the catch and mend their nets. The rest of the men loved to talk big by the pre-dawn campfires and tell their stories while cursing at each other before another day on the sea commenced.

Rina still had his eye after all these years. He knew she would be betrothed soon, and he had to make a life for himself if it were going to be to him. She had grown into quite a beautiful woman. She loved him; he was sure. If she had a choice, it would be him, but any dutiful father would make sure she did not marry for love but security.

Several suitors already had their eyes on her. Her lack of interest seemed to make them even more convinced that they would win her over. Ezekiel would have to act soon.

Such thoughts made his head swim in a dream while he was supposed to be selling fish at the market.

"Ezekiel! You have customers! I don't pay you to sit around!" said Hezekiah, the merchant. "I'm docking you twelve mites. If I didn't know better, I would think a girl was on your mind. Take it from me. That would be trouble. "

Ezekiel caught a smile from the aged fisherman-turned-merchant as he tended to the customers bargaining for the day's catch. He knew Hezekiah would not dock his pay. The man had lost a son to leprosy when the child was a boy of eight years old. Ezekiel became a sort of surrogate, and the feeling was mutual. He admired the man as the hardest working person he knew. Life had hardened the exterior, but Hezekiah had kept his heart protected.

He always looked after Ezekiel's family, bringing the day's leftover catch from time to time and making sure they still had enough food. Sometimes, it was leftovers from his stand that kept them alive. The pickling of sardines using old wine seemed to infuse Ezekiel's whole body with a smell that would repulse even the lepers. However, he was grateful for the work. Fishing was a rough but lucrative occupation. Selling fish in the market was not. He was barely able to make up for the lack of his father's income. It left little time for friends or leisure.

Rina seemed not to mind the smell and visited him every few days. Her beauty allowed her particular social graces that were not permitted to others under the Roman or Jewish law. Being friends with a man certainly had its drawbacks, and they had to be very careful.

The day seemed to speed up as the work was hard and demanding. With each incoming order, Ezekiel felt a fair wage becoming more and more secure. His mother affirmed him daily that working hard was a way to overcome the curse of his father's lack of responsible ambition.

His grandfather, Elyam, bragged about him to the other villagers, saying Ezekiel got all the good from their side of the family and none of the bad.

When the sun began to hide behind the horizon, Hezekiah brought out his scales and weights.

"I'm sorry, Ezekiel. There are no fish left to take to your family. However, you made a good day's wage, and I'm sure it will make up for the lack of musht." He smiled as he weighed the coins and divided the portion for Ezekiel.

"Don't worry about that. We have some leftover from yesterday."

"Your mother has made some baskets for me today. Please bring them tomorrow. We almost ran out with the fishing being so good lately."

"I'm considering going out and spearing tonight. The shallows are teeming with sardines."

"Be careful. Thieves are usually out at that time."

"I won't carry anything valuable."

With that, Ezekiel turned to walk the path to his home. The air smelled fresh as he left the market and walked along the seaside. Merchants set up small carts on the side of the path where Ezekiel could buy bread and a small pouch of wine. It would still be a good night with his family. Rina's family was coming to dine with them as they occasionally did since the day of the Roman soldier incident. When Rina's mother noticed their blossoming romance in the shadows, the visits became less frequent. She did not appreciate the son of a thief having eyes for her daughter. Even though Ezekiel had an incredible work ethic, the fear for her daughter's future was a strong impulse, kept in check only by Rina's father, Hadwin.

The thought invaded the recesses of Ezekiel's mind. He hurried home. Once there, Aaliyah baked some bread, put the grapes from the vineyard on the mat in the middle of the floor, and set the food in bowls made of olive wood. The smell of the pickled sardines warming on the clay oven filled the air with expectation as the guests arrived. Ezekiel always loved having guests.

The evening was lovely, and the families ate together as a cool breeze swept in from the sea. One subject was always off the table—Dismas. It was as though he never existed. The shame of the one who left his family was too much to bear.

As the evening meal ended, everyone clambered up the ladder to the flat roof to see the stars. It was a bright desert night. After setting down the mats and building a fire, Ezekiel wondered at the beauty of his muse and how the firelight danced off her delicate features. Her dark, curly hair reflected the light of the stars, setting a glow about her face. He could tell she felt him watching her, and she was comfortable with it.

"Rina, would you like to go for a walk?"

"I'd like that very much." A smile spread across her face as if she were just waiting to be asked.

"Mother, I'm going for a walk with Ezekiel."

"Be careful. Please stay close. If there are—"

"I know, I know. If there are any Romans, walk the other way."

"I'm just trying to protect you, child."

"I know, and I appreciate it. But I'll be with Ezekiel. I'm sure he can protect me."

Her mother furrowed her eyebrows.

Ezekiel led Rina to a small beach beside the sea. They walked in silence then fell naturally into conversation.

"I always like coming here. It's a great place to think and dream. Especially on nights like this."

"It's pretty," said Rina. "Who is that over there?" She pointed to a figure who built his fire right on the beach.

"I met him in the fish market. I think his name is Yeshua. He's a carpenter and also a Rabbi."

"Strange combination. Does Yeshua come here often?"

"I have seen him here once or twice."

"Do you know where he lives?"

"No, I'm sorry. We didn't get that far. Yeshua made a table once for our fish stand. The people in Galilee say he has an excellent reputation. His father, Yoseph, was known for his handiwork as well."

"Ezekiel, have you ever wondered about the future?"

"Many times. If I'm lucky, I will get my own boat. I really don't have a career that my father passed to me, but I had an uncle who was in the business, and I could learn it pretty fast."

"Your future wife may not like the fact that you smell of fish all the time."

"I'll figure that out when the time comes." He smiled.

"I guess what I mean is, do you have a plan, or do you just take each day as it comes?"

"Well, I like to think that if I'm supposed to do something, then it will happen. If the gods will it."

"Gods? You're Hebrew. We only have one God."

"Yes, but I've been thinking. What if the Romans are right about there being more than one god? I mean, I think our culture is the only one that believes in one true God who made everything and is in control of everything."

"I can't believe you're saying that. Do you know how much trouble you can get in?"

"Yeah, but only if you say something. You won't, will you? I'm just being silly. You do know that?"

"I certainly hope so. I'm concerned you might lose your direction," said Rina.

"Why?"

"Well, you know."

"I know what?"

"Ezekiel, you know I care for you. I just want to make sure you know you have roots."

"Well, not really. Ever since my dad's disappearance, I wonder if I should follow anything he stood for. He's so committed to his cause that he forgot he had a family."

"Your mother never talks of him?"

"No. She was so hurt that even the mention of his name brings up emotions she would rather bury."

Rina looked at Ezekiel with her deep brown eyes. "What about you? Are you alright?"

"Yeah, I'm always alright … never better." He smiled.

"Well, I'm here for you, if you need me."

Ezekiel nodded.

"I guess we better head back. Your mother will think something is up."

"At this point, I think she's hoping for it. She likes you, Rina."

"My family likes you too, but they would like us only to be friends, if you know what I mean."

"Who said anything different?"

"You did."

"I did?" he asked.

"Yes, in the way you look at me. The way you smile at me. It's all very scandalous," she said with a twinkle in her eye.

"I don't know how to respond to that."

"I'm just trying to embarrass you a little. You're my best friend, Ezekiel, and who knows what the future holds?" She grabbed his arm as they walked back.

CHAPTER 3

The sun's rays peeked from behind the animal skins covering the window of their clay hut. Ezekiel slept better than he had in a long time. It was the day before the Sabbath, and there was much to do.

"It looks like you and Rina are getting close." His mother looked up from the food she was preparing.

"Just friends, Mom."

"You may be telling yourself that, but my eyes tell me different. Please go slowly. You have very little to offer her. Please find a life first, then a nice girl. If Rina is still around, great. But you would do her very little service if you try to marry her now."

"Who said anything about marriage? We just went for a walk."

"You forget, I was young once. Walks turn to passion quickly. I just don't want you to get hurt when Rina is betrothed to someone wealthier than you."

"I know, Mom. You always tell me that. I will make a life that is better for all of us soon."

Ezekiel relished the Sabbath from sundown to sundown the next day. For a young man who worked tirelessly, a day of rest was not only sacred but welcomed. The time of silence and reflection seemed to repair the recesses of his soul. The only real action of the day came from the Romans, who respected the Jewish customs to keep the peace. So, Galilee's streets were quiet, and the shops looked like rows of shut eyelids, napping through the afternoon sun.

He could hear the families in their houses singing and passing the time with stories of high adventure. Grandpa Elyam had an endless number of stories he would tell. Each one ended with a twist that left the family laughing, even on the hundredth telling. Today, however, he was spending the Sabbath with his sister's family in Jerusalem.

The quiet allowed Ezekiel to mull over a plan. After five years, his father would not be coming back for the dagger. Ezekiel imagined him dead. The blade was worth at least eight boats. Ezekiel could build quite a life for himself with that many boats—a life that realized his every dream. He could have all his loved ones under one roof, safe from the uncertainty of the future. Ezekiel could sell the dagger and make Rina his bride.

He felt as though sundown would never come. When the sun finally slipped below the horizon, Ezekiel took his oil lamp and went to the olive tree, where he had buried the dagger in a small wooden box. The ground around the tree roots was compacted and hard. He had to take a rock from nearby to break the ground before digging with his fingers. After a few moments, his fingers hit something hard. Anticipation swelled in his chest, and he began digging harder. Patches of the wooden box came into view. Lifting it from the ground, he peeled the beeswax seal off the lid. Inside was the dagger, still glistening as if it were made moments before. He quickly hid it in his cloak and walked back home.

In the morning, he would find a merchant who knew its worth and would buy it for a fair price.

The next day, the market was bustling with merchants eager to make up for the lost day of the Sabbath. Some of them were poor and would have worked seven days a week if it were socially acceptable. Others were greedy and wanted their underlings to make them money every day. Still, most everyone accepted the law, if for nothing else than fear of shame.

The fish market would not open for several hours to allow that morning's catch to come in. This gave Ezekiel time to find the right merchant, then find the right carpenter to build his boats. The first merchant he came to was Eliab. He was a friend of Elyam and the family.

"Eliab, I have something to sell you," Ezekiel said with a definite note of caution.

"Come to the back here, young man. I'm intrigued."

"First, I need you to swear to secrecy. I can't let people know what I have."

"I swear upon my family's name that I will keep your secret. If I buy, I will simply say I found it on one of the street rats who no doubt lifted it from someone of means."

"I don't know much about it." Ezekiel produced the box from under his cloak.

"It's a beautiful piece. Greek, by the look of it. It must have come from someone important. Can I ask where you found it?"

"On the shore by the Roman docks. It must have fallen off someone's horse as they were traveling."

Eliab raised his eyebrows in suspicion. "How long have you had it?"

"Five years."

"Well, that's long enough for whoever lost it to give up on it. I can give you five hundred drachmas for it."

"It's worth at least nine hundred."

"You see, here's how this works. You found it, and now I found it. I could turn you in to the authorities, or I could give you a fair price for the dagger."

"Or I could let people know how you were dishonest with me and see if they believe me. The price is nine hundred."

Eliab laughed. "You're going to make an excellent businessman, Ezekiel. Nine hundred it is." He counted the coins into a bag and handed them to Ezekiel, who counted them again in front of him.

"You insult me, thinking that I would cheat you."

"You insulted yourself when you tried to cheat me at the beginning of this exchange," Ezekiel countered. "Do you know a good carpenter in town?"

"Yes, I've never used him before, but Yeshua comes highly recommended."

"Where can I find him?"

"He's from Nazareth. I hear he is honest and does good work. I also hear he is tough like you. You should get along just fine. He has a shop where his father once worked at the north end of town by the sea, just a short distance from Nazareth."

"You know, I've met him before. He built a table for our fish stand at the market."

"See, it must have been destiny then. Good luck and give Elyam my greetings."

"Alright, thank you. I will."

Ezekiel headed directly for Hezekiah's stand. When he arrived, he found the older man setting up.

"Ezekiel? I wasn't expecting you until much later today. I can't pay you much if you come early. The catch this morning is not going well, and I don't know if I'll have anything to sell."

"Well, in that case, I could use the day off, if you wouldn't mind."

"Take all the time you need."

"Thank you." Ezekiel then left to find Yeshua.

When he arrived in the northern part of town, the streets became very busy, making it difficult to catch the attention of a passerby.

"Excuse me, do you know where I can find Yeshua?"

The man just shrugged and kept walking.

"Excuse me, can you tell me where the carpenter Yeshua is?" This time, an older man pointed to a little structure on one of the side streets. Ezekiel adjusted his cloak and set off.

"Hello?"

"Hi, Ezekiel! Or do you not want me to call you Ezekiel, since we're not officially friends yet?"

Ezekiel looked puzzled.

"Well, if you want me to build these boats, you might want to say *something*."

"How did you know?"

Yeshua laughed. "You know, I never get tired of seeing that look on people's faces."

"So . . . will you take the job?"

"No."

"Why not?"

"I think you already know the answer. You were entrusted with a stolen dagger by which you came into this money. If I take the money, knowing it was stolen, I am no better than the one who stole it. If I build you these boats and do not have the means to return the dagger or the money, it will result in someone very close to you being put to death. So here is what I am prepared to do. I will build you one boat free of charge, if you return the money to keep the dagger safe until its owner comes to retrieve it."

"Eliab must have told you I was coming."

"Eliab has never met me. What he told you is true. He is also honorable. If you return the money, he will return the dagger to you. But you must go now."

"I could just find another to build my boats."

"You could."

"I need to think about it."

"I see."

Ezekiel walked away slowly, looking at the ground. He would find another carpenter. He did, however, choose to go with only three boats at first. This way, he could build up to the eight-boat fleet he wanted. His thoughts quickly turned to Rina. The only chance for a future with her was this. Once again, he asked around the market for a carpenter willing to build his fleet. He found him on the coast mending nets and fixing boats with pitch.

"Hello there," said Ezekiel.

"If you've come here to collect taxes, I have nothing to give you. My boat has been out of commission for seven days, and I've barely scraped up enough money to fix her."

"I'm not a tax collector."

"In that case, my name is Simon. What can I do for you?"

"I heard that you not only fish but also build boats."

"I've built a few. How many do you need?"

"Three."

"Three boats are going to cost you, my friend."

"I have money. How much would you charge me?"

"One hundred and fifty drachmas per boat, and you provide the wood."

"I can have someone else do it for one hundred, and they provide the wood."

"Then have them do it."

"Alright, I will." Ezekiel turned to leave.

"Wait!" Simon called. "I'll do it for one hundred and thirty drachmas."

"One hundred and ten, and no more."

Simon looked him in the eye for a moment. A smile came to his lips.

"I know you need the money. One hundred and ten is a fair price for any boat."

"Yes, I need the money. But understand you're not just getting any boat for that price. You are getting the finest vessels ever to sail the Sea of Galilee."

"How long will it take?"

"About three months. I can have them sooner if you pay me more."

"I will pay you half now and half when the boats are finished. I'll be by every day to check on the progress. I will help if I need to, but they must be done in that amount of time."

"I understand, my friend. I'll begin right now by purchasing the wood."

"See you tomorrow." Ezekiel counted out the money before his trek back home.

CHAPTER 4

Day after day, Ezekiel visited Simon while he worked on his boats. Within a month, the frame boards were lashed together, revealing the shape. The process fascinated Ezekiel. The smell of pitch and freshly hewn wood filled his nostrils as the planks were nailed in place and shaped by Simon's skillful hands.

Toward the end of completion, Ezekiel took a few days off from the fish market. Simon needed to dry the cedar wood by the fire and coat the boats inside and out with pitch. Ezekiel manned the pots of boiling pitch so each boat would be watertight. It was hard, backbreaking work, but Ezekiel liked it, even though he came home smelling more pungent than usual. He could see what was accomplished. It was more satisfying to watch a hull take form than to look at empty baskets of fish every evening. At each sundown, the boats became darker with thickening layers of pitch.

"So, how about the rest of the money?" Simon asked.

"You'll get it when the boats are tested."

"It will take a week for the pitch to dry fully. I can do no more as of now. I need the money."

"You will get the money when they are tested, no sooner," replied Ezekiel.

Simon shook his head as he picked up his tools. "Are you sure you don't have Roman blood running through your veins?"

"I'm Hebrew. Like you."

"No, you are nothing like me. Come, let's go and find some fishing nets for your new boats."

Ezekiel smiled as he went after Simon.

The market was slowing down as Ezekiel followed Simon through the winding streets. They came to a net and tentmaker of Samaritan descent. His face was pitted, and a scar, shaped like a jagged dagger blade, adorned the right side of his face.

"Simon, my friend. Have you come here to cheat me again?"

"Not this time, old man. I found some younger blood to do that for me. This is Ezekiel. He's decided to get into the fishing business, though I don't know why."

"I have my reasons," Ezekiel stated.

"You're impudent, Ezekiel. That's a good first step," replied the Samaritan. "So where did a young rat like you get the money to buy boats and nets?"

"That's my business, not yours."

"It's my business if you're going to buy nets from me with stolen money."

"It's not stolen money."

"I wish I could take your word for it, but it's been my experience that only the best proof is what the Romans rely on these days." He pulled his right arm from under his cloak, revealing a stub where a hand should be. "So telling me is not enough, I'm afraid."

The Samaritan looked closely at Ezekiel.

"Sir, I need nets, and you obviously can't use nets. I propose the less you know, the better. You can't be held accountable for something you don't know."

This brought a smile from the Samaritan. "You remind me of myself at your age. I think six talents for each net is a fair price. There are no finer fishing nets in all of Galilee."

"I'll give you four."

The Samaritan laughed. "No, my boy, my price is firm. If you don't like it, then you can find someone else in town who will give you a better deal. I don't need your money."

"Then we're done here."

"So be it," the Samaritan replied with a sober nod.

Simon pulled Ezekiel outside. "What are you doing?"

"What am I doing? We could go before the Pharisees for going into his house."

"It was the best deal you could find."

"I wouldn't be caught dead bartering with a Samaritan!"

"And what makes you so different? You think I don't know that your father was a thief?"

Ezekiel just looked at him.

"That's right. I did a little digging. You insulted my friend. There may come a time when you need him. He may be a Samaritan, but he's connected. Rest assured, if you ever do need him, he won't be there for you now."

Despite Simon's words, Ezekiel felt he was right. He decided to shake it off as he walked through the market to find another net maker. The shops, however, were about to close. After Simon said his goodbyes, Ezekiel decided to call it a day. He walked the familiar path back home, feeling good about the progress made.

He would see if Rina was home and if she wished to walk with him. Coming to her house, he was greeted with a warm smile. Rina was covered in flour from preparing bread for the evening meal.

"Mother is in the other room. You shouldn't be here, you know."

"All the same, here I am."

"I just denied another suitor. Mother thinks I'm foolish. But I'm not ready to settle yet."

"Even with me?"

"Look, Ezekiel, I don't see a future with us. As much as my heart tells me to be with you, I must honor traditions. And, well, you don't even have money for a dowry."

"What if I told you I did?"

"Then I would have to question how you came into such an amount of money."

"I've been saving up."

"Really? Working at a fish market stand, you've been able to make enough to pay a dowry and sweep me off my feet? Ezekiel, I like you, but even my faith isn't strong enough to believe that one. Why don't you take me as your friend for now?"

Ezekiel searched her face. Was she afraid? Did she like him? He said in a low voice, "If I were to get this sort of money together and build a life, would you want to be in it?"

"Look, I care for you very much. And in some ways, I might even love you, but you and I both know that it's impossible. I'm sorry. But I have to take a suitor sooner than you could get the money or a life together."

"Come with me. I have something to show you."

"I can't right now. Can we talk after dinner? I'll meet you near your spot if Elyam is back." She breathed a quiet sigh of relief to herself. She had almost slipped and said *our spot.*

"I think he decided to move to Jerusalem, but I will see if he is coming back," said Ezekiel. "I can meet you there anyway." Rina turned and left.

Ezekiel nodded as he walked away. The east wind seemed unbearable under the weight of the unknown. His walk home had never seemed so long. Each memory of growing up on the Sea of Galilee had Rina in it. Somehow, the world made sense when she was around. He could not imagine a life without her. Her eyes smiled when he was around, and he took comfort that she seemed at ease with him in a way she never was around anyone else. It was understandable of her to desire security. For the very poor, security was a treasure locked in a glass chest—something seen but never felt. To their imaginations, a windfall of money seemed as tantalizing as the food of God's table. For Rina, her beauty was a currency that could be exchanged for a key—to unlock a lifetime of luxury. It would be a shame to throw it away.

Though he understood that perspective, Ezekiel saw things differently. He felt as though they had just heard an enthralling call to adventure—as if some kind-faced king had charged them with a priceless dagger of his own making. It seemed that now Ezekiel and Rina stood at a cliff. He looked on as she considered casting the blade to the rocks, to the gnashing teeth of the tide, for fear it was secretly cursed. He hoped, as only a young man can hope, that she realized the promise of security—not their love—was secretly cursed, for no dowry, or marriage, or any other mirage of security could protect her from life's sandstorms. Ezekiel had learned that lesson the day he finally accepted his father would never return.

As he walked home, with her decision still uncertain and their cliffside moment suspended in time, Ezekiel felt that spirit roiling in his stomach again. He feared to lose the most precious thing he had laid eyes upon, and he imagined her standing in the doorway, freshly ground flour clinging to her palms. He remembered how a single lock of hair had escaped from her headscarf, lifted by a soft wind. The moment, vivid now in Ezekiel's memory, felt like a good omen urging him forward. That playful lock of hair seemed to whisper a promise: "If you choose wisely, one golden evening, you will watch her take down every strand on her head—the day of your wedding." Emboldened, Ezekiel channeled his energy into saving what stood to be lost forever. His love for her was an awakening, and there was no chance of falling back asleep.

"Slow and steady will win," he told himself as he neared his door.

"You don't smell of fish today. That's a welcome change!" Aaliyah quipped, setting a place for dinner. "It's just going to be the two of us today."

Ezekiel kissed his mother on the cheek as he got ready for a meal of lamb, grapes, and bread. "It smells wonderful, Mom."

"I know you won't be here forever, and I would like to spend a little time with my only child."

"I'm not a child anymore. I'm twenty years old."

"You will always be my child. And, yes, I know you're a grown man. I haven't told you enough how proud I am of you." This made Ezekiel smile.

"You didn't deserve the lot you were handed, and I will forever live with the guilt in my choice of husband."

"You didn't have much choice in the matter."

"That doesn't make the feeling go away. Just please tell me you'll be careful in those boats you're building."

"How did you know about that?"

"I may have been foolish with love, but I am no fool when it comes to my son. I hope you're not in debt."

"I'm not, Mom. I've been doing extra work to pay for the boats. I hope to have the nets soon."

"I have no doubt you will make a great fisherman, but I worry about you. Please be safe."

"I'm always safe. Sometimes I think I try to be too safe."

"Those are the comments that worry me."

"Don't worry. I will always be around to take care of you." Ezekiel smiled at his mother's scowl.

They ate in silence for the rest of the meal. As they cleaned up, Rina announced her presence before entering the house.

"Rina, I didn't realize you were coming over tonight."

"Sorry, Mom. We're going for a walk, but we'll be back before too long, alright?"

"If I refuse, would it make a difference?"

"You won't refuse, and I love you for that."

"Hmm."

"Don't worry. I'll make sure he's safe," Rina said sweetly.

Ezekiel smiled, and they made their way onto the street.

"I didn't think you would come."

"Well, I couldn't talk there. Mother was in the other room listening to our every word."

"So, were you lying back there when you told me you need security more than love?"

"No, I wasn't. Look, my heart says one thing, but my mind is telling me there are other options. I care for you, Ezekiel, but I have my entire family to think of."

"Is there someone else?"

"There's one suitor who's trying to get me to agree to marriage. He comes from a wealthy family, and my family would want for nothing as long as they lived if we married."

"Do you love him?"

"I can learn to."

"I wanted to show you something that might change your mind. However, if you've already made up your mind, then it will be worthless."

"I haven't made up my mind yet," she said.

"So, do you want to see it?"

"See what?"

"It's a surprise." Ezekiel winked.

"Well, lead the way!"

He took her along the shore to where Simon worked on the boats.

"I'm learning the fishing trade, and these are my boats."

Rina looked puzzled. "How could you possibly afford this?"

"I recently came into a lot of money."

"By dishonest means, no doubt."

"No, not at all. I just sold something and . . ."

"What? What did you sell?" she interrupted.

"Just something my father left me."

"So it *was* by dishonest means."

"No, it wasn't."

"I need to go, Ezekiel."

"Well, wait, I—"

"Don't say anything else. I cannot marry a thief."

"I'm not a thief!"

"Your father was. Anything he gave you was stolen. If you sell something that was stolen, then you are no better than the thief." Rina walked away.

Ezekiel was so taken by surprise that he didn't bother going after her. He kicked the dirt in frustration and returned home.

This was his future. There was no way he could attain it without the promise of a career. He was lucky. He could just as easily have been a beggar on the street. But this was an opportunity he could not pass up, even for Rina. He wouldn't give up on her. She just needed time to think about things.

The next few months passed in a slow and painful march of time. Ezekiel began his fishing career. The bounty was plentiful, and he prospered. He soon hired a crew of eight, then twelve. It wasn't long before his name grew in stature among the regions—a young man who'd made something of himself from so little. It was an act of godliness to create something out of nothing. To some, he became a hero. Others looked upon him with suspicion and jealousy. Ezekiel took it in stride as he worked hard six days a week, sunup to sundown.

CHAPTER 5

R ina still refused to marry. She wouldn't marry just anyone, and she tried to remain friends with Ezekiel. His marriage intentions suffered her more grief than she let on, yet she refused to let her heart go easily, finding herself continually drawn to this upstart son of a thief. He was like a well that looks shoddy in the distance but reveals itself to be deep and reliable when you come near and plumb its depths.

On a bright blue morning in the middle of the week, another well presented itself on the shifting horizon. Asher walked through the streets of the market with his mother and sister. Despite the hustle of the market, he walked as though he had no care in the world. Asher held his head high, not in the off-putting, cocky way of someone trying to prove himself, but in a certain way that showed he knew where he was going. If you observed him, perched overhead on a rooftop or balcony, you would see how the crowds seemed to part before him naturally—unconsciously, even—as he wound through the thickets of patrons and merchants.

He tossed dates, one by one, into his mouth as he walked. When she saw him, Rina looked up and away. He noticed, and Rina blushed. Her heart dropped like a smooth, heavy stone in the ocean. He was, in both looks and demeanor, incredibly attractive.

"Hello," he said.

Rina looked up to see a set of perfect teeth, a sight as rare as a string of pearls. Above, the smile in his eyes was even more disarming.

"Oh, um . . . hi?"

"I don't believe I've seen you around here before."

"I live on the north side of the city. I don't come to this part of the market very often."

"Well, that explains it. The name is Asher."

"That's a unique name," said Rina.

"It means happy. My parents wanted to have joyful children, so they named me Asher. My sister over there is Abigail, which means—"

"My father's delight," Rina interrupted. This brought an even bigger smile from Asher.

"I'm Rina. It means a song of joy."

"In this instance, I think the Arabic meaning suits you better."

"What is it?" she asked.

"One who is beautiful."

"You are too daring."

"So, I'm told." Asher smiled.

At that moment, they heard a woman cursing at a vender. "This is the worst produce I've ever seen. These dates are rotten. How could anyone let you sell such horrific fruit . . ."

Asher rolled his eyes. "My father's delight indeed!" He looked at Rina as if to say, *I've got to take care of this.*

"I've got to go," Rina said, almost knocking over a basket of fruit. She blazed a trail through the people and didn't stop until she was home.

CHAPTER 6

Fishing was hard, and Ezekiel loved it. He wore his exhaustion proudly at the end of each day, like a piece of fine clothing. He slept as deeply and silently as an underground cave. Each morning he woke naturally before dawn, never once hesitating to break from the cocoon of his mat into the cold morning air. The energetic way he tossed aside his swath of bedlinens, still warm from wrapping him through the night, almost seemed callous. He was, however, merely young and brimming with purpose.

Life on the water was aggravating. Every task was subject to the weather, and the central job—netting a large school of fish—sometimes seemed like a game of pure luck. As fishermen are among the most superstitious people, that was a testament to how fickle the trade could be. One thing was sure, however, he loved the influence he had gained over the fishermen, once they saw he treated them fairly. Each wage was balanced carefully using honest scales. His crew became like a family. On the fifth day of each week, Ezekiel would send his fishermen elsewhere while visiting each of his merchants. He soon learned that relationships were the stuff of good business. He made sure each merchant was reputable as well. On this day, as he made his rounds, he came upon the carpenter hut where he first met Yeshua.

Ezekiel had the time and decided to pop in. It would be good to see the look on Yeshua's face since he was doing so well. Unfortunately, the carpenter was out. *I'll have to catch up with him later*, he thought.

"Ezekiel."

He turned to see Yeshua returning with an armful of short logs.

"I wish I could say I'm glad you're doing well."

"Because it means you were wrong?"

"No, it means you didn't heed my warning. The heavenly response to your choice will shake the very ground you walk on. But I tell you," Yeshua continued, his eyes locked soberly on Ezekiel's, "I tell you the truth, if you persevere, you will find happiness again."

"What is that supposed to mean?"

"You will know soon enough."

"How will I know?"

"You came here to tell me I was wrong. And now you ask yourself whether I'm right. My dear Ezekiel, your heart is conflicted. You love a woman who questions whether she can love you back. So, you sold a dagger that was not yours to build a fishing operation for yourself. You're in a hurry to get to a future that you may or may not want."

"How do you know these things?"

"That's not the right question. The question is: If I know all this, what else do I know?"

"I don't understand."

"See this block of olive wood? It started its life as a tree. When it was too old to bear much fruit, it was cut down. Then it was cut into pieces. For it to be useful again, I will get to the heartwood. The bark is stripped away, and the natural beauty of the wood comes to the surface. Then it must be smoothed and shaped into the bowl or beam or paddle or mast. None of which can happen if it is left to rot. Look at me, Ezekiel. Life is going to do the same to you. Don't let it beat you into meaninglessness. You'll have to excuse me, now. I have to get back to work."

Ezekiel turned to leave.

"And one more thing. The answer you're looking for is yes."

"Yes?"

"She does love you." Yeshua smiled and began chiseling.

Ezekiel nodded politely and left.

The next day was like any other. Ezekiel woke up and went out on his boat. His fishermen worked hard for the next eight hours, hauling in load after load of fish. The market was flooded with travelers, and people loved spending money this time of year. Ezekiel smiled as he ended the day by salting the fish for the next day's market. Afterward, he swam in the sea to wash off the muck. He felt grateful the sea continually changed its colors, that it was fickle and made his work difficult while keeping its promise of remaining ever new. The shade of difference between yesterday and today was always clear to fishermen. They paid attention to the details that expressed the novelty of that chameleon called הווהה, or "the present." As Ezekiel returned to the gently sloping bank, his eyes alighted on the figure of Yeshua, waiting patiently where the water met the Promised Land.

"How was your day today?" Yeshua asked as Ezekiel emerged from the water.

"You should already know. You seem to know everything about me already."

Yeshua smiled. Ezekiel made his way out of the water and quickly donned his cloak.

"Well, I wanted to hear it from you."

"It's been a good day in one respect and not so good in another."

"That would be yesterday."

"Yes."

"Ezekiel, I would love for you to be one of my followers, but I already know you'll turn me down."

"Why do you say that?"

Yeshua just smiled as Ezekiel looked at him glaringly.

"You are really into fishing, huh?"

"Yes, it's the life I have chosen," Ezekiel responded.

"What if I told you I could make you a fisher of men?"

"I would say you make no sense."

"Exactly. Have a good evening, Ezekiel." Yeshua left to walk down the shoreline.

"Go tell Simon that fisher of men thing. He would probably fall for something like that."

"He already has," Yeshua called back.

Ezekiel rinsed his feet off in the water and ran his fingers through his matted black hair. The sky faded over the countryside in a brilliant display of red, yellow, and purple. Ezekiel took a moment to enjoy the view before he headed home. The gentle wind felt cold on his back. He held his head high to compensate for the emptiness in his heart. He was learning to hide his emotions well. Heartbreak and pain were constant companions and had been for quite some time.

CHAPTER 7

R ina could not get Asher out of her head, and, consequently, she lamented her foolish behavior at the market. What if he came calling for her? Should she give up hope that Ezekiel would become someone who could give her a future?

Asher's so handsome, she thought, *but it feels like a betrayal to Ezekiel.*

She couldn't just think of herself and her suitors, however. Her family's future was tied up with hers. How would it look to marry the son of a thief? She lay on her mat, wondering what it must be like to lie on cushions. What feeling came with owning your own horse? She drifted off to sleep in a sea of emotions.

The next day, Rina's father, Hadwin, returned from his work in the vineyards. He worked at the adjacent vineyard where Rina's mother picked grapes. His job was to oversee the wine presses and account for the wages of the workers. It was honest work, and Rina admired her father.

He liked Ezekiel, which was a wonder to Rina. "Life is hard for the rich just as it is for the poor," he used to say. He was a hardworking man of few words and a kind smile. He somehow escaped the bitterness that harsh times seemed to lay on men his age.

"Father, how was your day?"

"It was a good day."

"You say that every day."

"Yes, I know."

"Why don't you ever say more than that?"

He just smiled and laid down his satchel.

"This is what I mean. You don't even answer questions sometimes."

"If I don't have an answer, why would I give one?"

Rina chuckled. "You see? This is why you're in charge of all the workers. They know you won't inflame the emotions of the laborers."

Hadwin just smiled. Rina went about her housework. She was glad her father was home. His presence made her feel secure.

"A young man was looking for you today in the market."

"Oh really, who might that be?"

"He looked rich. Sorry, though, I didn't ask his name."

"I met someone the other day. He's really handsome, but I'm not ready to settle down yet."

"You're running out of time, Rina."

"Abba, I'm only twenty-three."

"Most women have been married for six or seven years by now. What's holding you back?"

"I like my life right now. I don't want it to change."

"My dear Rina, life always changes. The sky has never been the same color twice. The life you dream of does not exist. Just find a nice young man and settle down. I would like to know my grandchildren before I die."

"Well, if I wait, maybe you'll be motivated to live longer."

He laughed briefly then fell silent.

Rina heard the familiar sound of feet crunching the gravel outside the door. Ester walked in.

"I concur with your father. You need to find a man as soon as possible."

"Mother, I will not rush into this."

"Then you will die an old maid with nothing to show for it."

"Maybe that's what I choose."

Rina's father nodded to Ester to quiet her.

"You're always placating our daughter. Perhaps if you had a stronger hand with her, then she would come to her senses."

"It's her decision. Our daughter does not exist for us. We are entrusted with her care until we can give that over to a man who will then take care of her."

"Humph!" Ester stormed out the back doorway.

"Thanks, Daddy," said Rina softly. He just smiled.

"I want to know a little bit more about this young man."

"I only met him once. There's nothing there."

"Well, he seems to think there could be. How is Ezekiel?"

"Why would you ask?"

"Because you've been fond of him since you were young. Have you spent any time with him lately?"

"Why do you like him so much? Mom thinks he isn't worthy as a suitor."

"What do you think?"

"I still think about Ezekiel. As far as Asher goes, he's handsome. And he has the appearance of someone who's well off."

"Who makes you happy?"

"I'm extremely attracted to Asher, but I feel at ease with Ezekiel."

"Alright."

"That's it? Just alright?" Rina looked at him in disbelief. "How can you offer no solution?"

"I've learned that people can talk themselves into the right decision if given the right amount of time. They can also be talked into the wrong ones by those they love."

"How did you know Mom was the right match?"

"She knew before I did. I think she had me picked out and placed herself in situations where I would notice her. She didn't have to. I noticed her right away and fell in love with her spirit. What can I say? It worked."

"I kind of feel that way about Ezekiel, but I fear he's not honest. I love him, but I cannot bring shame on my family by marrying the son of a thief."

"A man is not always as his father is."

"But what if he turns out to be?"

"Love is always a risk. Do you hope for the best when you're with him?"

"Yes, always."

"Then it's your choice."

"Well, I don't want to rush."

"Then, don't rush. Your mother and I want the best for you. That's all."

"Thank you, Dad."

"I know you'll make the right decision." He smiled his infectious smile once again.

Rina hugged Hadwin and went about her housework. Her head swam with all the possibilities. It had been some time since she imagined a future without Ezekiel. Now Asher, who fulfilled every fantasy of love in her head, showed up asking for her company. She had other suitors who thought they could woo her, but her thoughts always stayed true. She didn't know if she could fully trust Ezekiel. Maybe it was providence. Maybe Yahweh was showing her something better.

CHAPTER 8

A sher asked around to find where Rina lived. The only information he gathered was where her father worked. He made the trek to the vineyards. The immaculate farms were a testament to Hadwin's leadership.

Ordinary laborers do not yield these kinds of results. Maybe he would buy the vineyards. His family owned several others farther north. It could be a good business decision.

He walked the paths around the field where workers were building and repairing trellises for the new plants. The fresh air filled his lungs. What a welcomed change from the city where the smell of people lingered. His freshly oiled black hair twisted in the breeze, which felt cooler since his visit the day before. He loved the winemaking business.

In truth, it wasn't the business he loved so much as the wine. His position allowed him to taste wines from all over the world. His newest taste for the fermented drink came from the newly acquired Roman territory, Germania, called mead. It was made from fermented grain and honey. Asher sought to bring this drink to Israel's children by introducing it to the Levites, who could leverage it against the people. The Levite priesthood made their influence substantial.

Mead was stronger than wines of the day and would fit well with the Hebrews' bitter pallet. He could build the fermentation bins right next to the wine presses and pay some of the workers an allotment of mead in addition to their wages. The addition of honey and wild yeast made it more intoxicating. As soon as the public took notice, the region would be rich with the beverage.

With a little imagination, Galilee could be a cultural center of the region, he thought. The area could use the creature comforts of Rome. He could marry a local and take other mistresses as well. This would endear him to the people and let him make a name for his family, which his father would be proud of. In that sense, Rina was a perfect match.

He was attracted to her beauty, and he would also have the Hebrews eating out of his hand. Asher was half-Roman, half-Hebrew. His father married a Roman, which was a mark of shame on his extended family. However, the favor he carried with the Romans was more than worth the slight, yielding trade agreements that would have been impossible otherwise.

This day, he walked among the workers, inquiring who owned the vineyard. Since his father had been sent to the leper colony outside of Jerusalem, it was up to Asher to keep his family name alive. The task felt like a heavy burden.

"You there! Do you know who owns this vineyard?" he asked a man carrying a basket of nails.

"Yes, sir. His name is Eber from the tribe of Judah."

"Where might I find this Eber?"

"He lives in Tiberias near the springs. He doesn't like visitors. He's a good master, though. We are well paid for our work."

"How then would you suggest that I contact this man?"

"He goes to the market every first day after the Sabbath. If you ask people, they will point him out to you."

"Thank you, sir."

The man nodded back and went about his work. Asher mounted his horse and rode into Tiberias straight away. *Business cannot wait.* Along the way, he decided to stop by Rina's house. The day was waxing hot, and she might provide him with some refreshment. He rode hard down the road to her home. Rina was thrashing wheat to make bread.

"Hello. I wasn't expecting to see you today."

"Surely you know I've been asking about you."

"Yes, I heard," she said.

"I was wondering if we could get some water and talk for a while."

"That would be disgraceful. I just met you, and there are no family members around."

"Then you can serve me as your guest."

"I suppose that would be alright."

Asher dismounted his horse and followed her into the house. Rina pulled the animal skins off the windows and left the door open.

"You know, you are much too daring."

"You said that before."

"I know, and I mean it," she replied honestly.

"Rina, my intentions are true."

"Yes, but I wouldn't know that, would I?"

"I'm a man who knows what he wants. I admire true beauty, and I have traveled extensively to find it. Let me just say I have never witnessed a woman as beautiful as you."

"This is why I say you are too daring."

Asher moved toward her.

"That's far enough." Her voice was less than convincing as he pulled her close and kissed her. He felt her relax in his arms, then, as suddenly as the kiss started, she pulled away.

"Don't do this. Not now. It's forbidden."

"Alright. I'm sorry. I don't know what came over me."

"Don't be sorry either. Just slow down. I have a lot to consider before allowing myself to be swept away."

Asher nodded, slowly left the house, and mounted his horse. He smiled at her before galloping off. It was a game he had played many times before, but only when he traveled outside of Israel. It was too dangerous to do so without intentions to marry her. The Sanhedrin would have the poor girl stoned, and he could be fined.

No, Rina would do. She was poor enough to bridge the gap of public opinion, and she was Hebrew, which would make the Sanhedrin happy. The Romans could care less who he picked. His Roman citizenship through his mother ensured good relations there. All in all, Rina would be the prize of his new business venture.

His horse's hooves fell syncopated and steady against the ground. In his travels to the Orient, he had heard of a concept called Zen, a kind of mindfulness that comes from thinking nothing while sensing everything. The rhythm of horse and rider always pulled him into such a state. Riding was one of the great pleasures of life. The steed was magnificent and brought admiration wherever he went. Asher decided to make the horse open fully down the lonely, dusty road. The beginnings of a clopping echo resonated through the hills. By the time he made it to Eber's house, the horse was gasping so hard Asher thought he might collapse. He chuckled to himself as he dismounted. The door was made of cedarwood and bronze, which was as imposing as Eber's reputation.

After shaking the dust from his sandals, he proceeded to the door. Before he was able to reach it, a voice boomed, "Who goes there?"

"My name is Asher, and I'm a Hebrew. I am here to inquire about a price for the vineyards just west of town."

"They're not for sale. Go away."

"Isn't that for your master to decide?"

"Aren't you being a little rude?"

"Depends. If I buy the vineyard next to it for a fair price, your master loses a deal because of you."

"Wait here." The door closed with a creak. Moments later, the door opened again. This time the servant was accompanied by an older man, short of stature and bald.

"My servant tells me you're interested in buying a vineyard. You are wasting your time."

"Once you know what I offer for the vineyard, you might reconsider."

"Well then, come in, and let's hear this amazing offer."

The dichotomy of the house's exterior and interior was striking. The interior was decorated with relics from all over the known world. Asher recognized Indian art as well as African tapestries. One thing was missing—Roman art. This man was most likely a Zealot sympathizer, and maybe Asher could play to his political leanings.

"I have some tea from Asia. Would you like some?"

"Yes, thank you. I haven't tasted the beverage since my travels to the Orient."

"So you are well-traveled. What keeps you in Tiberias?"

"Several things. I want to settle down and make a life that is my own."

"I take it you come from a wealthy family."

"Yes, my father was a Jewish prince."

"That's interesting. I don't know too many Jewish princes who have any wealth left since the Romans tax them so heavily."

"There are always ways to hide one's wealth. Especially if one does not claim it all at once."

Eber furrowed his bushy eyebrows. "So, I take it you are not exuberant about the Roman occupation."

"I'm an opportunist. If I can thrive in this environment, I will. If I can make money from them, then that's what I will do. I have contacts and have built many relationships with the Romans. However, I am not in favor of what they have done to our people."

"Spoken like someone whose wisdom is twice that of your age."

"My father was killed trying to fight with the Zealots. They never knew who he was, or I would be imprisoned. My mother is Roman. Since my father was Hebrew, I felt this would be a great place to start." Asher felt the lie leave his lips. He reveled in his ability to shape the winds of his fortune. "Where does your allegiance lie?"

"With ambition. I think the Romans are filthy swine. They are unfit for anything except to feed the ocean. I know one must be careful when talking around here. The walls can have ears. But you are safe here."

Asher measured his words. He didn't want to be too bold, but he knew if he could find common ground, the vineyard would be his in no time.

"I hate them too, but my life gives me no quarter for such hatred. I simply cannot afford to hate them, at least for now. Your secret is safe with me."

"It's no secret. Let the Romans come for me."

"You are foolish if you think they won't."

"I don't need a lecture. Let's get down to business," Eber said.

"How much are you willing to pay for the vineyard and winepresses?"

"Three thousand gold talents."

"The price is five thousand."

"It's not worth five thousand," Asher responded.

"You said you had a great offer, and yet you come up short. The price is five thousand."

"I will pay you four thousand and not a drachma more."

"You insult me with such an offer. The lowest I will take is four thousand five hundred talents."

"Done. I will have one of my servants bring the money tonight under the cover of darkness."

"Just meet me tomorrow with the money. We'll let the workers know they will be working for you from now on. Please treat them fairly, as I have."

"You have my word. Tomorrow, sunup."

Eber nodded. "My servant will show you to the door."

"It was a pleasure."

CHAPTER 9

E zekiel arrived home to find his mother silently working the dough with her fingers. The flour seemed to hang in the air. Ezekiel coughed, and Aaliyah promptly stopped to wipe her forehead with the back of her hand.

"How did the fishing go today?"

"It was fair. I made enough to pay the fishermen. I have some leftover to help here. I'm even able to save a little. Soon, I'll ask for Rina's hand."

"Well, I hope you will be happy with her. She's a wonderful woman." Aaliyah forced a smile.

"What's wrong, Mom?"

"Nothing. It just seemed like yesterday I was teaching you how to walk. Now you look as though you are ready to take on the world. Just don't forget your mother when you make your fortune."

"You know I would never do that." Ezekiel winked at her and put down his satchel. "What's for dinner?"

"Your favorite. Lamb stew with bread. I'm tired of fish."

Ezekiel smiled as he helped his mother prepare the table.

That night Ezekiel laid on his mat and wondered what the future would hold. The business was going well. Still, there was a restlessness that besieged him. His mind kept turning over Yeshua's words. *Fisher of men.* What did that mean? Apparently, a recruiting strategy, but for what? He couldn't think of anything, unless Yeshua was a Zealot.

If that was the case, Ezekiel wanted nothing to do with him. His thoughts turned once again to Rina. It seemed she was never available anymore. The pit of his stomach turned. His thoughts twisted like vines, always searching, keeping him awake. He would have to make his move soon.

CHAPTER 10

Rina couldn't shake the feeling she was cheating on Ezekiel. Her situation was both exciting and nauseating. Ezekiel would make a good husband but would never be able to pull her family out of poverty. Plus, he hadn't been completely honest with her about the curious origins of his money. She had trusted him her whole life, yet he would not give her a straight answer. Asher, for better or worse, had no history with her.

He was a clean linen with no stains, and that was refreshing. Plus, he was exceedingly handsome. Their children would be beautiful.

I owe it to myself to see where this goes, she thought. Her girlfriends would approve of Asher over Ezekiel, but she was over the flighty ways of youthful girls.

Love was a luxury, but one she craved. She knew Ezekiel would love her, but could Asher? She wasn't sure she was really attracted to Ezekiel, but she loved him the way one loved an older brother. Her head swam with the possibility of Asher, but her thoughts always turned to Ezekiel. This war in her heart plagued her thoughts until sleep finally overcame her.

The next morning, she woke with a start. Sunlight peeked from behind the date palms just outside her window. The burlap curtain let just enough light in to hurt her eyes as she stretched her arms and rolled off her mat. It was going to be a busy day. Her work was never done, and her father needed help in the vineyard. One of the workers had been kicked hard by a donkey in the mouth. The work had to get done, and the only one Hadwin could trust to pick up the slack was Rina. She knew it was an honor to have such trust from her father. And since Asher was asking about her at the vineyard, it would be a chance to see him again. Dread filled her stomach, while elation filled her chest.

She walked behind her father all the way to the vineyard, keeping the mandatory five steps behind. From the looks of how things were going, she would have to work harder than anyone else merely to save face. It would help her father, though, and he was a man worth helping. She knew she would be safe as long as he was around.

It was a beautiful morning. Rina couldn't help but have lifted spirits. The work in the vineyard was arduous, but the soft morning sun made the task bearable. Today's task was pruning the vines, and each worker had a bronze blade used for shearing the unwanted tendrils. The work gave Rina a needed reprieve from the inner turmoil she felt in her heart.

Her father knew she could outwork any man on the crew, and the day became a competition. Rina loved challenges, and, in a way, she relished the fact that grown men were insecure about being beaten by a woman.

The heat of the afternoon waxed intensely, but Rina seemed not to mind. Everyone worked as hard as they could. The other women looked at her as an inspiration. Rina smiled as her section was cleared quicker than everyone else on the crew. She then turned her attention to helping the other women on the crew finish their plots.

It was a record day in the fields.

She couldn't help but notice two men talking near the presses. Her heart leaped into her chest. *Asher.* But who was that with him? It seemed to be an older gentleman. Then it dawned on her. *That's Eber.* She caught Asher looking her way and averted her gaze.

Although the end of the day drew near, Rina kept the furious pace as if the workload demanded it. The other workers slowed down to enjoy the cool of the shade and tally their progress. This fact did not go unnoticed by Hadwin, who quietly walked into the field.

"Rina? It's time to come in," he said gently. Rina's cheeks turned red as she gathered her things and went into the storehouse for her final tally. The wages were weighed, and her father gave her the half measure reserved for women. He kept her other half measure under his cloak to make things fair when he returned home. This bothered Rina. She didn't like special treatment. Other women were given the half measure for their work and were happy to work at all. Rina knew it wasn't fair, but this was their world. No one was going to change it. At least, not in the foreseeable future. She loved her father for trying to be fair but resented the situation.

Reasoning with him was futile. He would say the same thing each time: "The men are not worth as much to me." Eber knew about the arrangement. He let it slide because he depended on Hadwin's leadership abilities.

Rina wondered what Asher was doing with Eber on the hill. Was it business? Was he there to see the workers? Was he asking about her?

After work, Rina walked home. On the way, she stopped by an old olive tree. She had never thought much about it, but today it seemed to have more character. It reminded her of her childhood when Ezekiel would climb to the top of every tree just to make her nervous. He was always showing off. The thought brought a smile to her face and overwhelming sadness in her heart. He would never live up to what she needed. Asher would make her life comfortable. The choice should be simple.

She moved on before tears escaped her eyes. She noticed movement to her right just off the path. It was a lamb. The baby was stuck in a thicket of briars. It had black spots, so she knew it was not being held for the Day of Atonement. She went over and gently picked up the lamb and held it close.

"Where did you come from?" she said aloud. There was no brand, so she decided to take the lamb home, to the small pen behind their dwelling, and find out to whom it belonged. She also knew anyone could come along, and the lamb would become a meal. Compassion overwhelmed her. She felt lost like this little lamb.

CHAPTER 11

E zekiel prepared himself to go to Rina's. He finally had enough money for a dowry and could provide a life for her. The thought brought a smile to his face as he looked out the window. The sun glowed a tangerine hue, which meant she would be home from the vineyards.

Thump, thump, thump. He could hear his heartbeat pounding in his ears as he mustered the courage to take the next step of his life. He prided himself on being a planner, charting every step with the tools he was given. A group of children played in the street with sticks for swords. Roman children were easy to spot with their traditional white togas contrasting with the burlap and animal skins of the Hebrew children. Young women were helping their mothers by watching the younger children. Roman soldiers seemed to pay little attention as they engaged in their talks of war and adventure. Ezekiel almost envied them and the experiences they had. He had never been outside of

Tiberias. It would be nice to see the world. It would be even nicer to see it with Rina.

Finally, he could see her house in the distance. Smoke curled into the air from the fire opening. They were cooking dinner. He smiled as he walked. Surely, he would be invited for dinner. As he neared the abode, he noticed a man on horseback riding to the house from the opposite direction. Puzzled, Ezekiel quickened his steps. He stopped at Rina's house. Rina came into view, and it was as if a tunnel formed around his eyes, centering on Rina and this man. She was smiling. Her eyes danced the way they once danced with him. It was like watching himself from outside his own body, only he had been replaced with a better-looking version. Moments later, Rina noticed him walking the path toward them. Ezekiel halted. There was no more to say. There was nothing to do at that moment. He stood there with his gaze upon the one who broke his heart.

"Ezekiel, I want you to meet my friend Asher and his sister Abigail."

He seemed not to hear her.

"Is he dumb?" asked Abigail.

"Ezekiel?" asked Rina.

"Oh. Hi," he said at length. "I'm sorry. I must have interrupted something."

"This isn't what you think it is."

"Can I say something here?" Asher asked.

"What?"

"I think this is exactly what he thinks it is. Unless you were lying when you kissed me the other day."

"Aw, brother, you are so cruel," said Abigail in a mocking tone.

Ezekiel filled with rage. Before he could control himself, his fist crashed into the face of his rival, sending Asher backward to the ground. Abigail backed up in amazement then in one swift motion turned and mounted her horse and galloped away.

Rina screamed, "Stop! Are you an animal?"

"You made a big mistake. You just attacked a Roman citizen."

"You've dishonored my friend. I believe it'll be you who will pay."

Climbing to his feet, Asher looked Ezekiel in the eye. "You know I could make you pay for your insolence, but since you're Rina's friend, I'll overlook this infraction. On one condition—you never call on her again. Think carefully about my offer. I can make you and your family pay for what you just did."

"Is that a threat? Because the way I see it, I was defending Rina's honor. I could say the same to you. Leave her alone."

"Both of you stop," Rina insisted.

"I can explain this. I just purchased a certain vineyard, and it provides you with a life, Rina. Doesn't your father have a position of authority there? I was coming to talk with him about a little matter of the heart. It looks like I was almost too late," Asher said.

Ezekiel said nothing for fear his temper would get the best of him again.

"So, here's my offer. Rina, I'd like you to be my wife. If you accept my offer, then your father will be put in charge of another vineyard I own. If you don't, I can't promise anything, but I think I may look for more loyal subjects."

"So, she's just a piece of property you can barter for?" Ezekiel stepped up to Asher, but Rina stopped him.

"And another thing—I won't have Ezekiel thrown in prison for his crime."

Rina felt the heat of anger rising in her soul. "So, if I agree to marry you, you won't hurt my family? Are you insane?"

"Am I to take that as a no?"

"The way I see it, I can just say I saw you force yourself on her," Ezekiel threatened.

"Who are they going to believe? A fisherman or a wealthy Roman? As a Roman citizen, it's within my rights to take a wife of my choosing from any of the girls of our conquered empire."

"No, it's not." Ezekiel glowered.

"Again, who're they going to believe? It's well within my rights to strike you down right here. After all, you attacked me. In fact, I think that's exactly what I'll do." Asher went to the scabbard of his horse and pulled a sword. He smiled at Ezekiel's retreat. "I knew you'd come to your senses."

"So you're saying that if I agree to marry you, you will keep my friends and family safe?" Rina asked.

"Yes, provided I don't have to defend myself again," said Asher.

"Can I think about it?"

"Don't think too long." Asher mounted his horse and rode away.

"Rina, you don't have to do this!" Ezekiel said.

"You attacked a Roman citizen, Ezekiel! His family is well-connected, and he just bought the vineyard where my father works."

"Roman citizen or not, I'll defend your honor."

Rina frowned. "What if defending my honor dooms us all? Then what? Are you just going to challenge him?"

"Even a Roman citizen has limits on what he can do."

"Not to us. They can do whatever they want, and we have no voice."

"I have a voice."

"And your arrogance is going to get everyone killed. I have no choice. I have to accept his proposal."

"Some proposal. *Marry me or I'll hurt everyone you know.* Do you think he's capable of being a loving husband? You might live in luxury, but make no mistake, he'll abuse you and move on once he's done," said Ezekiel with disgust.

"And what of my parents? What of you?"

"I can take care of myself. As for your parents, there are always other vineyards."

"I'm sorry, Ezekiel. There's no other way." Rina walked inside, shouting, "Don't follow me! I think it's best if we part ways."

Ezekiel stood there in shocked silence. Surely, she didn't mean it. He walked away after a moment of reflection, knowing it would be fruitless to try speaking with her now.

People gathered on the street, speaking so loudly Ezekiel couldn't focus. All he wanted was to get away. He wanted to run. He wanted to take one of his boats and brave the sea—to reach a new land with a new promise. One thing stopped him, however: his hatred for his father.

Just then, the seed of a plan hatched in his mind.

CHAPTER 12

bigail rode into the Tiberias market. She had no idea what she was looking for. Just something to buy and the thrill of irritating her brother, whom she loathed. After tying up her horse at the entrance, she stepped into the crowd. Slowly walking by each of the booths, she ignored the vendors who were trying to sell her new garments or fruits and grain. She saw something shiny in one of the booths, and her heart sank to the pit of her stomach. She had seen this dagger before. It was stolen when she was a teenager—intended to be delivered by her father in exchange for a land deal in Jerusalem. Since her father was murdered and the dagger stolen, they had to settle in Tiberias instead.

"How much for that?" she asked. Eliab stood to attention.

"This is a very nice piece," said Eliab, who brought the dagger from its display stand.

"This piece was stolen. I demand to know who you bought it from."

"Just some street rat who picked it up from the streets."

"I don't believe you. I'm going to ask you again or I will bring my family in and you can tell them. My father was murdered for this dagger."

"I paid a lot of money for this piece. I had no idea it was stolen."

"Give me a name and I will pay you thirteen hundred drachmas for it."

Eliab pondered for a moment. "You can't say I told you."

"Your secret will be safe with me."

Again, Eliab paused. He didn't want to betray Ezekiel, but he needed the money, and if the dagger was stolen there was no way he could sell it.

"Money first."

Abigail produced a money pouch from under her garments. She set down the sack full of coins on the table, allowing them to clank for effect.

"Name!"

Eliab's face fell somber. "Ezekiel."

CHAPTER 13

The room seemed strange to Ezekiel. A peculiar haze filled the space at the edges of his vision. In the center stood Asher and Rina in a passionate embrace. Asher withdrew a dagger from her abdomen as he stepped away. Blood soaked through her outer garment as she fell to the floor. Asher turned his gaze to Ezekiel with a devious smile and laughed triumphantly. Ezekiel ran toward Rina, who turned into Yeshua with the prophesy, "Someone will die if you don't return the money and retrieve your dagger."

Ezekiel's eyes flew open. His cloak was drenched in sweat as he stood from his mat. The room was silent as he walked into the night air. The dream etched newfound resolve in his mind.

Why would Yeshua show up in a dream, though? It had been almost two years since he heard that prophesy. He searched his mind for another way but couldn't think. Like a tattoo on his mind, the thoughts consumed him. He would have to find Eliab.

Word reached Hadwin that Rina was considering a proposal of marriage to the man who would become his employer. The news grieved him. He knew she had always dreamed of marrying someone she loved. Though it seemed irrational to him, deep down he knew marrying for love was a thing of the future, and the currents of time were against his daughter.

Rina sobbed at the thought of marrying Asher. She needed to decide soon. She hated seeing her father work so hard and knew he would take an early grave if he continued at this pace.

On the other hand, Asher's threat was a window into his soul. She hoped it was just an emotional outburst, but he had seemed so cold, so calculated. She felt like a piece of land to be bartered for. In that moment, all the attraction she had for Asher transmuted into fear.

She had hoped for clarity by this point, that her thoughts would stop turning to Ezekiel. Though she was trying to protect him and her family, she felt ashamed for entertaining the idea of Asher's proposal. How could a man speak of love then talk of her as if she were property? But she knew—to men like Asher—that's all women were. Property. She was fortunate enough to have a father who was a good man. He had taught her the value of independence, so, when a man came along, she could truly have freedom within the relationship. Now she was to be a slave. Like her grandmother, she would live in the confines of society and marry for survival. Tears fell from her cheeks like falling stars. It was the death of a dream.

The next day, Rina woke from a deep sleep. Somehow, she was just as exhausted as the night before. Her dreams had fallen dark with the night. The smell of bread baking in a clay oven just outside filled her nostrils. The sweet aroma of fresh honey collected by her father was also a welcomed scent of home. Rina wondered how much longer she would have before she was whisked away to serve a master whom she now found repugnant. Still, the smile of her mother warmed her heart, and she remembered why she had to do this. Her loved ones must never know of her sacrifice. It would be her and Ezekiel's secret. In the meantime, she needed to get a message to him.

"I need to go for a walk, Mother."

"Alright, I'll go with you."

"No, I need to go alone."

"Alright. Please be careful. You're my only child. I wish I could give your father a son, but all he has is you. It would break his heart if something were to happen to you."

"I'm always careful, Mother." Rina kissed her on the cheek and hurried out the door.

Fighting back tears, she ran to Ezekiel's house. Once there, she saw no one was home. Ezekiel must have been out fishing. She had to see him, although the pit of her stomach turned in fear that she would be found out. Tears made streaks in the dust accumulated on her face. *I must look like a wreck*, she thought.

She went past the animal skin door and looked for some way to get a message to him. Her Hebrew was impeccable. Her father taught her every night when she was little. He thought it would make her a more desirable wife someday. She found a remnant of dried animal skin and a crude cooking knife. She took the end of the blade and pricked her index finger. She willed herself not to make a sound and wrote in Hebrew the following words with her blood:

It read, "You must know what I do, I do out of love. There has never been someone whom I have loved more than you, my dear Ezekiel. But now I must love another. Please forget about me with the knowledge that you did the best you could."

Afterward, she washed her hands in the sea. The message would be received. She had let him down easy.

"What are you doing here?" said a voice from behind.

Startled, she turned to find Aaliyah. "I just left a message for Ezekiel."

"So, I saw. Let me see your hand . . . You know we have ink. You also know Ezekiel has loved you since you were little. If you think you can leave him without it hurting, you're mistaken."

"I'll hurt him and everyone else I love if I stay."

"Rina, there are ways of becoming a slave while thinking you're doing the right thing. I thought I was right to marry Dismas, and it brought me nothing but pain. He seemed wealthy, but I didn't really love him, at least not at first. When I found out what he was, it was too late. There was good in him, but the bad won in the end."

"I won't be marrying for money. I'll be marrying for the security of those I love."

"They say love is only for the Gentiles, but their marriages are just as bad as ours. It seems love is a myth, but then I see your mother and father. I realize if you find something like that, you fight for it."

"Aaliyah, I love your son. That's why I must leave. I can't explain it, but I hope one day you'll understand."

Aaliyah hugged Rina with tears in her eyes. "You know you are like a daughter to me. Please don't do this. But even if you do, I wish you never-ending happiness."

Rina was speechless. This was the kind of mother-in-law she always hoped to have. Now it was all out of reach. The more she tried to push it out of her mind, the more it rooted in the core of her heart.

CHAPTER 14

W hen she arrived home, Asher was waiting for her.
"I was hoping to have an answer by now. Surely you've had enough time to consider my proposal."

"Asher, I was attracted to you, yes, but I'm not property you can barter for. You threatened my family and dear friend. It is not something easily forgiven." Rina knew she must weigh her words carefully. For now, she didn't want to seem eager to push him away.

"At least understand I do what I do because I love you."

She looked at him for a moment, not knowing what to say. Her lips parted, but words were slow to come out.

"So you threatened the people I love because you love me? I don't understand."

"Oh, I stand by my threats, but it's only because I have to have you."

"Then I'm not an object of your love, just your obsession?"

"I take it your answer is no," said Asher.

"My answer is yes if you keep your end of the bargain. However, I have some caveats of my own. You honor your promise to keep Ezekiel safe. You give my father a raise with the ability to buy the vineyard. And I want you to pay a dowry worthy of the woman who will give you an heir."

"Do you think you're worth it? With a flick of my hand, you and your family could be enemies of Rome."

"We would be *free* enemies of Rome. If I were to marry you, my life would not be my own. I would be your trophy—brought out whenever you wanted to show me off. I could live with that if those I love are safe. You say you love me. I'm worth at least that."

Asher smiled up at the sky. "I believe I've met my match. I love a cunning woman."

"And one more thing. We do this with a Hebrew wedding and engagement. Nothing Roman involved. Understand?"

"I understand. I understand you're not in a position to make any demands, but these seem to be reasonable, so I'll comply. See you later, my love." Asher smirked as he turned to leave. "One more thing. I need you to attend a party with me in three days. I'll have the garment makers come by and measure you. There will be important people there, and I need you to make me look good."

Rina said nothing as Asher caressed the side of her face.

"Your coldness toward me will have to change. But don't fear, your father will receive your dowry within two days. Everything you requested will be done. Now excuse me, I have some business to attend to."

CHAPTER 15

Ezekiel put away the nets for the day as he and his fishermen dragged the boats onto the beach. The day's catch was abysmal. Each cut was barely enough to live on.

"Hopefully tomorrow will be better," he said to Simon, who ran the crew.

"I have something I want to talk to you about."

"Alright."

"Several of us have decided to follow Yeshua. This will be our last week working for you."

"I know."

"You do?"

"Yes, he approached me too."

"Then you're coming with us?"

"No, I don't believe I will."

"Why not?"

"Everything I have, I built for myself. I want my life to be good, honest. I don't want to go around listening to some philosopher about a kingdom that exists in the realm of fantasy. I'm a good Hebrew, and I make sacrifices. I keep the commandments as best I can. It has to be enough."

"But haven't you ever wanted to be a part of something bigger? I look at Yeshua, and I know there's more than catching fish."

"He used the fisher of men line on you too, huh?"

"As a matter of fact, he did, and I believe him. Ezekiel, I want this. I hope there are no hard feelings."

"Of course not. I hope you find the happiness you're looking for, my friend. You will always have a job here."

"Maybe our paths will cross again."

"I certainly hope so."

The day fell dark as the men went home, leaving Ezekiel there to mend his nets and his broken heart. He didn't walk directly home as he did most days. He went for a swim in the sea, letting the gentle waves lap over his cheekbones as he floated on his back. Every muscle ached.

The next morning, Ezekiel woke up on the beach. He didn't remember falling asleep or even walking on shore for that matter. The color drained from his world. He needed to work, but he couldn't find the courage to keep going.

It wouldn't hurt to have a day off. He could send his workers out for the day's catch and work with what came in.

Along the path, vendors were trying to get in on the action before the market square. A beggar grabbed the front of his garment. "Please, I haven't eaten in three days." His accent gave him away as a Samaritan. In a move to appease the man, Ezekiel pulled out three shekels of silver and handed them to him. *He may be a Samaritan, but he deserves to eat.*

"Why don't you take him to eat with you?" came a voice from behind. Ezekiel turned to the easy smile of Yeshua.

"Oh! It's you."

"I have an idea. Why don't you treat all three of us?"

"I'm very busy."

"No."

"What do you mean, no?"

"As in, no, you're not busy."

"I'm busy being alone," Ezekiel responded.

"So be it."

"I don't need your permission."

"If you knew me, then you would understand how foolish that statement is."

"It's alright, really. I'll just be on my way," said the Samaritan.

"My friend," Yeshua said. "I want to spend some time with you. Ezekiel, what do you say?"

"Okay."

Yeshua smiled. All three went to a little stand and bought some sheep's milk and pickled sardines. They sat down by the sea and talked. Yeshua built a small fire as they lounged and ate together. They spoke for the next half hour, and Ezekiel noticed something. Yeshua didn't try to prophesy over him or command him to do anything.

This is new, he thought. The Samaritan sat there nervously listening to every word. Ezekiel felt a stirring in his soul as if Yeshua were an old friend he hadn't seen in a long time. Every question he asked of the Samaritan was met with a nervous laugh or a one-word answer.

Finally, Yeshua asked a question of Ezekiel. It wasn't a probing question, as if he wanted some juicy dirt on Ezekiel, but it seemed he truly wanted his opinion.

"What do you think of the newfound peace between the Levite Pharisees and Sadducees with the Roman occupation?"

Ezekiel, afraid to offer his real thoughts, gave a neutral reply. "I'm afraid I'm ignorant of such matters. I know the leaders are walking a thin line, and peace must be attained for the prosperity of our people."

"That's a well-measured answer. However, I'm interested in what you really think. Remember, Samaritans hate the Romans as much as Hebrews do."

"What about you?"

"I hate injustice wherever I see it. I love all people, and I hate when others are bent on causing suffering. Forgiveness is the only way forward. Otherwise, the fight continues, and no one wins."

"Talk about measured answers . . ."

"Yes, but this one, I believe. You don't really believe your answer."

Ezekiel paused for a moment, considering his audience. "I believe nothing good comes from Rome. I believe we Hebrews are losing our culture through this abomination."

This brought laughter from the Samaritan.

"You speak of your culture as if it were holier than everyone else's. I have seen abominations come, not from the Romans, but our brothers, the Jews. You cannot only see with your own eyes."

Ezekiel knew it to be true. Samaritans were half-Jews whose culture mixed with pagan practices, drawing the ire of the priesthood.

"Why do you pose such a question?"

"I'm beginning my purpose soon. I wanted to see what you thought."

"You already knew what I was going to say, though. How?"

"All will be revealed. On a lighter note, I have a party to get ready for."

"What kind of party?"

"A wedding party. Well—" Yeshua rose to his feet. "Have a wonderful day."

Ezekiel and the Samaritan followed his suit and said their goodbyes. The rest of the day went by too fast. Ezekiel felt even more tired from the day than if he had worked. He went home and laid down on his mat. Aaliyah stayed outside the house. She didn't want to disturb her son, so she went to her father's house and left him alone for the night.

The next day, Ezekiel went into town ready to fish as he did every morning. Youssef, recently hired to replace Simon, was packing the nets meticulously.

"Did you hear about the wedding last night?"

"No."

"Well, it was my niece who got married. The feast was amazing, but the bridal party severely underestimated the amount of wine that was needed. Then a friend of my wife, Yeshua, I think his name was, asked to do something. He instructed the master of the servants to fill all their cisterns with water. When they drew the water, it was wine. And not just any wine—the best any of us had ever tasted!"

"I know Yeshua. Simon, James, and John went to study under him. He's a rabbi and a carpenter by trade."

"It sounds unbelievable, doesn't it?"

"It sounds like the wine you had was a little too good."

"Think what you want, but it wasn't only me who witnessed this. Everyone's talking about it."

"Just help me get this boat into the water. Please?"

"Yes, sir," said Youssef as he garnered the rest of the men together.

As they pulled three of the boats away from shore, Ezekiel noticed Yeshua walking with a group of men along the beach. Simon was trying to keep people away from him so they could make progress. A crowd was gathering.

Ezekiel and Yeshua locked eyes for a moment. Everything around Ezekiel seemed to slow down as if time had stopped. The boat lurched and brought him back to the present moment.

It seemed strange to Ezekiel that so many people knew of Yeshua in such a short amount of time. He was odd to most people. He seemed to have special knowledge one would associate with a demigod or a soothsayer, yet his power did not seem to come from superstition or enchantment. He didn't speak in a language from foreign lands or use sleight of hand tricks like the people traveling from the East were so fond of.

It was his demeanor which caught people off guard. He was disarming in a way that allowed him to speak the truth without offense.

As the day lagged on, the work put Ezekiel's mind at ease. He had wanted to do this for Rina, now he would work for himself and his mother. It would provide a certain amount of satisfaction. He would someday find a lovely girl and marry. For now, though, he had to put her out of his mind. The market never rewarded the sluggard. His body was well-muscled from years of hard work.

In the back of his mind, he thought of his father. Would he be proud or disappointed? Ezekiel imagined he would be proud. He refused to be a disappointment like his father was.

As the last pull of the nets came in, Ezekiel decided to allow his men to fill the baskets for the market. Exhaustion swept through his body like a heavy stone on his chest. He needed sleep, but none came lately.

The men pulled the boats onto the shore and cleaned the fish in the shallow water. Ezekiel walked home, stumbling along the way. A vendor was selling wine in animal skin pouches. Never was Ezekiel so tempted to drink his mind into oblivion. He purchased the wine and drank it on the way home. It was an old wine with a stronger taste than the one he and his mother used to celebrate Passover each year. When Ezekiel arrived home, he fell to his mat and slept hard.

CHAPTER 16

Rina tried on the new garment in the Roman style. She would have to layer it with some of her other clothes to keep with the Jewish law of modesty. Rina had never seen a garment that was so white in her life. She gingerly slipped it on. Her mother had remnants of myrrh-infused oil, which she dabbed on her wrists and feet. The oil lamp sent a cascade of shimmering light across her face, highlighting her natural beauty. Her mother fixed her hair with the same myrrh-infused oil then prepared herself.

She smelled as pretty as she looked.

Hadwin met his daughter outside, faking a smile for her sake. "You will make a bride fit for royalty."

"Thank you, Papa." She blushed, and for a fleeting moment, her sense of dread melted away as she looked up to see a horse and rider leading another horse for her to ride.

"I'm Shalom, servant of the merciful Asher of the house of Micah. He instructed me to escort you and your family to the gathering. If you need anything, consider me your servant as well." He helped Rina onto the horse while he instructed Hadwin to take the other. Ester would walk behind with the servant.

Rina glanced at her mother, and a tear painted the corner of her eye as the horse clopped on slowly, allowing the servant and Ester to keep up. This lasted for the next three miles until they reached the palatial estate. Asher was there in his finest clothes of blue silk and clean linen.

Fine tapestries lined the walls of the stone building, giving the appearance of vast wealth. Inside were over twenty people of importance. Women and children were relegated to the background while the men lounged in the center of the floor, talking business and politics. Musicians were setting up their lutes and lyres and many kinds of drums Rina had never seen before. In one corner was a vat filled with a bubbly substance that had a faint resemblance to wine but smelled much stronger. Servants ladled the brown liquid into wooden cups and passed them to the men first. The men of Roman descent nodded approvingly as they drank.

"I see Asher has found a new prize for his desires," said a man before taking a big swig of his cup.

"This is to be my wife, and you will treat her with respect," said Asher.

"I'm sorry. I was just having a bit of fun. No harm intended."

"Well, drink up, my friends. This is going to be the new drink of Galilee!" He proceeded to fill his cup with mead and instructed the musicians to play.

The guests danced to the folk song while eating and drinking. The heaviness of the mead was entirely different from the wine the Hebrews were accustomed to. Hadwin spat his out and asked for wine instead. The more adventurous ones of the group drank with abandon. The effects of the alcohol slowed their movements and made them jollier.

Asher outdrank the entire group. Staggering to the middle of the floor, he raised his cup and proposed a toast to Rina.

"There's the most beautiful creature I have ever laid eyes on. She's spirited and will be a great accompaniment to all my adventures. May she bear me many children, and may they see the greatness of Rome and the great riches to be had. May the gods smile on our wedding."

Hadwin immediately rose and gave his own speech. "May they ever acknowledge the one true God of Ibrahim, Isaac, and Jacob. May they never bow down to foreign gods and remember their heritage!"

Asher, humiliated, staggered toward Hadwin as quickly as he could. "How dare you defy me in my own house! I will have your whorish daughter for my wife, and she will answer to me alone. If you want any part of her life, old man, you will denounce your speech as too much wine."

"Do you think I answer to you? Remember, you're only half Roman. Will you denounce your Hebrew heritage, just so you can sell this sewage water?"

Asher took two steps back and reached under his cloak. He lunged at Hadwin with a dagger. The curved blade was made as an instrument of war, good at slicing the necks of unsuspecting warriors.

With one motion, Hadwin sidestepped the younger man and pushed him into a clay pot, causing him to stumble. The dagger dug into Asher's leg, causing a crimson stain on his linens and silk.

The other men seized Hadwin and threw him out of the house. Rina was not far behind.

Asher slowly rose from his fallen position. He looked down at the dagger protruding from his leg. Wrapping his hand around it, he yanked it from his leg with a scream. The partygoers simply stared, not knowing what to do.

"Well, don't just stand there! Bring that whore and her father before me. They will be tried in a Roman court!"

"Weren't you the aggressor? You attacked that poor man, who was only defending his daughter's honor. Would you overlook his offense?" his sister, Abigail, asked in a low voice.

"You should remember your place!" He brushed passed her.

"And you need to keep your cool, or all your plans will dissolve like a pillar of salt. I like Rina. I think she could be good for you. Hadwin will ultimately bend to your will. Play along until you're married and then do as you wish."

"I can't let this injustice stand!"

"You won't. Just wait until you have her in your possession, then do as you please. Hadwin will rue the day he stood up to you, and Rina will learn to love you."

Asher knew she was right. He had to be patient. Then the room went black. The wound in his leg was bleeding fast, leaving a puddle on the floor. The men tried to bandage the wound but to no avail. The men carried him to his room.

His head burned with sweat as the blood slowly clotted to close the wound. Most left, and the few who stayed prayed to their gods for healing. One by one, they were allowed to enter the room where Asher lay fighting for his life.

Abigail asked to be left alone with her brother. Once everyone left, she stood over his pale, convulsing body. It was as if a weight had been lifted from her.

"For too long I watched you oppress the women around me. For too long I stood by as you sullied our name. You are just like our father. I cannot say I'm glad you're on death's door, but my heart cannot and will not mourn for you, brother. I fear if you're to live, our family will suffer more of the same." She took linen fabric and placed it over his face, pressing as hard as she could until she felt the life drain from his body.

Taking an oil lamp, she held it close to her eyes. The burning oil irritated her eyes enough to induce tears.

"He's dead," she cried in a voice loud enough for the household to hear. At once, her mother and the rest of the men rushed into the room. They confirmed his death.

"Hadwin must pay for this," Abigail said in a small voice. Years of abuse had hardened her heart toward her brother. She only hoped her feigned grief was convincing. Now she was heir to the family fortune and, with her mother, would rule the vineyards and live a comfortable life.

CHAPTER 17

Hadwin packed all he could on his three donkeys as Ester and Rina worked furiously to gather enough of their belongings to leave town. They left within the hour, headed toward Jerusalem.

"Do you hear that sound?"

"Yes," said Ester.

"It's the sound of men coming after me. You two need to go on ahead."

"You cannot leave, Papa," Rina cried.

"Listen, Rina. I need to face the consequences of my actions. You go ahead. If I can, I will meet you in Jerusalem. If I don't, then you will know I'm dead. Wait no less than one year, then come back and look for Ezekiel. I'm sure he will take you for his wife and look after you and your mother well."

"Do I have a say in any of this?" Ester asked.

"My dear, I want you to know I love you. Protect our daughter." He dismounted, tied his donkey to Rina's, then set off.

"Papa! I can't let you do this." Tears streaked down Rina's cheeks.

"I told you to go! Your mother needs you. If you come with me, you and your mother will die."

"I don't think I could bear to lose you."

"You won't. Now go! This is my wish—that you and your mother will be safe."

Hadwin walked in the opposite direction. Regret filled his heart and mind regarding his actions with Asher.

I will try to make the best amends I can and beg for mercy. The inky darkness seemed to swallow the light from his oil lamp. Ahead, he saw torches and heard a voice barking orders. It was the voice of a woman. He snuffed his lamp and carefully moved closer. He recognized Asher's sister with all the servants. Each one carried a sword. Immediately, Hadwin understood. Asher was dead, and the party was headed in Ester and Rina's direction. He had to create a diversion.

"Hello there!"

The group of servants turned around. Bringing their torches forward, they soon illuminated Hadwin. A tear fell from his eye as he threw his staff to the ground.

"I'm not armed."

The servants quickly surrounded him. His first thought was to make a run for it. However, it occurred to him there were enough witnesses to come to his defense. He decided to see where this would go.

"You killed my brother! You will die according to Roman law," Abigail said with an affected note. The hatred that should have tinged her voice was missing.

"I don't know what transpired since I left, but everyone here knows what I did was in defense of my family and myself. I did not attack your brother. He attacked me. Many of your servants know me, for I was their master in the fields. They know my character."

"Quiet! You will stand trial and be crucified for this insurrection."

"I didn't know a woman could bring such charges, or is Rome allowing your citizenship to overrule my Hebrew heritage?"

"Rome could care less what I do with you. You have no rights under their law."

"But I do have rights under Jewish law, and since you're Hebrew as well, you know they will not see your side of this. Especially since your brother was trying to pervert our customs with this witchcraft called mead."

"You speak well for a commoner . . . It will do you no good." She turned her attention to the servants. "If you care for your families, you must kill this man where he stands. I will not allow the blood of my brother to go unavenged."

The servants seized Hadwin at that moment, and Jeremiah, one of the men Hadwin knew, came forward.

He whispered in Hadwin's ear, "I'm sorry. I will try to spare your life with this blow." Suddenly, he thrust his sword in a glancing blow under Hadwin's tunic, so the blade drew blood but didn't hit any organs. Keeping his body between Hadwin and Abigail, he withdrew his blade. The blood flowed from the wound, and Hadwin made a convincing collapse. Jeremiah shook his head.

Turning to Abigail, who seemed as cold as ice, he said, "Let me bury this man according to Hebrew law, for he did not deserve the death you dealt him."

"Very well, as long as I never have to see his face again."

The other servants took Abigail back home while Jeremiah stayed with the body. Under the cover of darkness, Abigail didn't notice Hadwin was still breathing. Once the servants were out of sight, Jeremiah knelt beside him. He was in such pain he could no longer hold still.

"I—I know what you did. If this didn't hurt so much, I'd be thanking you right now."

"Hold your tongue! I have to carry you now. You could still die from your wound, but I know a physician in Galilee, and he might be able to heal you. Then you must leave Galilee forever."

Hadwin nodded. Jeremiah put Hadwin's arm over his shoulder, and, together, they hobbled into town. At length, he knocked on the door of his friend Luke.

"Who's there?"

"It's Jeremiah, and I have a wounded man here."

In a few moments, the door swung open, and Jeremiah carried him inside. By this time, Hadwin was sweating heavily and had the look of death about him.

Luke quickly dressed the wound with olive oil and frankincense. "By whose sword did this happen?"

"Mine. Although it was to save his life."

"Don't say you saved his life yet. He has bled a lot, and I don't know if I can stop the bleeding."

"Please do your best. This is a good man who fell into a difficult situation. I'll pay whatever you require."

"I know a man who might be able to save him, but I must go and find him now." Luke got his tunic and hurried to the door. He paused only to say, "Please, stay with him until I get back." Jeremiah nodded as Luke disappeared into the first hours of the morning.

Abigail went straight to her room and wailed. Her will to preserve herself had now sent her brother and an innocent man to the grave. She had managed to hold herself together until she reached her room. To the servants, she was merely grieving for her brother, but she knew the truth.

Under the cloak of darkness, Luke reappeared with Yeshua. By the light of the oil lamp, Yeshua placed his hand on Hadwin's forehead. Hadwin awoke in a daze.

"I want you to know your sins are forgiven. You are healed!"

At once, Hadwin sat up on his mat. A cool breeze entered the room.

"I don't understand."

"I healed you. Now go into the night. It's not safe for you to stay."

"What do I tell people?"

"I don't think you will want to tell anyone right now. Everyone thinks you're dead. You being alive could endanger your family."

"Can I follow you?"

"You don't have to walk with me everywhere I go to be a follower. Just keep my teachings, and you will be alright."

"Here are some clean cloaks," Luke said. "Put them on and don't look back."

Hadwin changed out of his bloody clothes and fled into the early hours of the morning. He hoped to make it past the city before he was recognized. With each step, his equilibrium improved as his body replenished the blood he had lost.

CHAPTER 18

Rina and her mother made it to the outskirts of Jerusalem. She regretted leaving without her father but knew his parting words to them were true. All she could do now was press on and pray for a miracle.

She would set about finding a new man to take care of her and her mother while in Jerusalem. But the task proved to be more difficult than she imagined. She worked alongside her mother in the grain fields outside the city, and they lived in a small tent she had purchased by bartering a few lambs. The harvest time made people excited. It was a time when the poor could glean the leftover grain in the field. Rina made baskets from reeds that grew by a nearby stream and stored the grain for the future. The grain would soon be the currency they needed to survive.

She regretted leaving Ezekiel without saying goodbye. Maybe she would send word when they could afford it. For now, she had to survive.

She hoped her father would turn from his foolishness. However, with every passing day, hope turned to despair as she knew the chances of his survival were slim.

Each time she thought about finding a new man, her thoughts turned to Ezekiel. She wondered what he was doing at that moment and if he thought of her. She would never forgive herself for the look on his face when she agreed to marry Asher. She had hurt her best friend.

———————

Ezekiel tried to push the situation from his mind. He focused on his work now that he was three men down. He heard in the market that Hadwin and Asher were dead. Rina and her mother were nowhere to be found. The crew noticed his grief and tried to console him, but to no avail.

The waves grew around the boats, lapping at their sides. Today, they only had two of the three boats due to the lack of fishermen.

"We need to lash the boats together," shouted Ezekiel.

"What did you say?" Youssef asked.

"I said we need to lash the boats together. It'll be more stable that way. Tell the others!"

Once the boats were tied together, they tried to wait out the storm, but it soon became apparent it would be suicide not to make it to shore. Raindrops fell heavy on their skin as the men tried to pull in the nets. One wave pushed Ezekiel off his feet, thrusting him to the stern. His men dropped the nets to help him, but over they went, leaving the men without the means to fish and Ezekiel with the task of finding new ones. They rowed toward shore and prayed the boats would hold together.

"What's that noise?" Ezekiel asked, alarmed.

"We're running aground!" said Youssef. "The boats are going to break up if we don't make them lighter!"

"What can we afford to lose?"

Youssef looked at him in disbelief. Usually, Ezekiel was the problem solver. "The rest of the nets and the fish we caught earlier."

Ezekiel's heart sank. That was his entire profit for the day and then some.

"How close are we to the beach?" asked Youssef.

"The wind has pulled us off course. We're in the mountain region. Near Chorazin, I believe. Where the Zealots hide."

"How do you know that?"

Ezekiel was spared from answering as another wave knocked him off his feet. The waves were getting stronger. He knew the boats could break under the strain as they rowed as hard as they could toward shore. Another wave crashed over the side of the left boat, pulling the bow under water.

Immediately, they realized the mistake of lashing the boats together.

The fishermen tried desperately to cut the lashing before both vessels sunk, but it was too late. There was an awful cracking sound as the seams split apart. Water filled both vessels while the men tried in vain to bail it from the boats.

Ezekiel found himself in the water, clinging to the chine logs of the boat. Another wave crashed over his head, splitting the doomed vessel in two. He decided to swim for it. Gathering all his courage, he let go and set out for shore. The other men were nowhere to be seen. They had most likely drowned. He fought to keep his head above water as the waves conspired against him. Then his foot hit the seafloor. He might just make it after all. He tried to stand, but the water was still up to his neck, and the waves made it impossible to walk to shore. The rain was coming down in sheets at this point. Ezekiel squinted to see the shoreline. Finally, the water was shallow enough for him to walk the rest of the way. His cloaks seemed to weigh as much as a ballast stone.

Once out of the water, he collapsed on the shore, allowing the rain to beat the briny stench off his body. Two boats lost. Possibly his men too. *They knew the risks*, he told himself. But as he looked up, he saw Youssef waving to him.

"Praise Yahweh, we are all here," he said in a strained voice.

Exhausted, Ezekiel just nodded and sat on a washed-up log.

"I think you were right. We must be near Chorazin. If we start walking, I'm sure we can find help."

"Let's find some shelter first and get out of this rain."

The men nodded in agreement. They plodded for the next hour toward the mountains.

"Is that a cave over there?" Youssef pointed toward a rocky outcrop, but when they reached the opening, he reconsidered. "I'm not sure this is a good idea."

"Why not?"

"Thieves use these caves as hideouts."

Ezekiel smiled while Youssef and the others grumbled. "You're supposed to be brave fishermen." He entered the mouth and disappeared into darkness.

The sound of an animal running split the rain's steady syncopation. Suddenly, an ibex ram ran through the opening toward the men. They were so startled that Youssef fell onto his backside, earning him a peal of laughter from the rest of the men. Ezekiel reappeared at the opening, grinning from ear to ear. The men needed a good laugh, and it was as though Yahweh was smiling on them once again.

For Ezekiel, the reprieve was short-lived. Responsibility for his men settled as a crushing weight on his shoulders.

The sun set behind the horizon, and the men decided to camp for the night. They made a fire while making up stories. It seemed to ease the tension of their situation. Ezekiel caught some locusts to cook on the fire, and they eased the pangs of hunger with the insects.

"You know, I hear there's this guy named John who lives on these things. He finds honey to help them go down easier."

"Nothing could make these things go down easy. Yuck." Youssef scrunched his face as he suppressed a gag reflex.

"When I was a boy, we didn't have much. My mother would mix them into the bread dough so it would be more filling. You get used to it after a while," said Nicodemus, the new hire.

"If you cook them on the rock by the fire, they become crunchy."

Ezekiel stayed quiet for much of the banter. His mother would be worried about him not coming home tonight. Why he cared, he had no idea. After all, he was an adult. He didn't have to answer to her for anything.

The crackle of the fire soothed his nerves, as did the smell of the burning wood. Sleep would soon be upon them. As his mind drifted, the men continued with their jokes and laughter. It made him smile that they could be happy after such an ordeal.

The night was miserable as his damp garments chafed his skin. He decided to get up and walk around some. By this time, the sky had cleared to reveal a tapestry of stars.

Is there really a God, and could He even care about me? The question infected his mind. Ezekiel tried to release the thought, for he had been taught the God of the Hebrews was the one true God, and if he doubted, he was guilty of heresy. Lately, he found it easier to believe in a pantheon of gods as the Romans did. It made sense. If there was one God, then why was there so much corruption? He would never admit this to his mother or Elyam. As far as they knew, he believed in Yahweh. But what had Yahweh ever done for him? The Romans lived so as not to offend the gods. They could do whatever they wished as long as they paid homage to the gods of their choice. It seemed liberating.

He returned and decided to let the fire dry out portions of his clothes, leaving him halfway refreshed and sticky at the same time.

Since learning of Hadwin's death and Rina's disappearance, Ezekiel felt lost. The way everything had played out, he didn't even get the chance to enact his revenge on Asher. The funny thing was, his death didn't ease his hatred of the man. If anything, he wanted to see his suffering. He wanted to watch as he took his last gasp of air, as the light of life dimmed from his eyes. Now, he was left feeling the void of the life he could have had. At that moment, he felt he had nothing left. The money he saved would go into buying two more boats. It wouldn't exhaust his funds, but it would slow his progress on making a comfortable living for himself and his mother.

The men seemed to sleep better than he did. He felt the temptation to leave them to fend for themselves. Of course, he wouldn't do that. He just wanted to run away—to end it all. It just seemed like he couldn't overcome the passivity overwhelming his spirit. It was a spirit dangerously close to being broken.

CHAPTER 19

When she and her mother had saved enough, Rina went into Jerusalem to sell the grain she had gleaned from the harvest. That day, she found an alley off the main street where there was still vacancy. While setting up her baskets, she heard a familiar voice.

"The price you've set for this oil is outrageous! I'll take my business elsewhere."

"The price is firm, old man. A lot has changed since your youth. I'm giving you a deal!"

"Hah!"

"Elyam!" Rina called.

Elyam turned to see the face he hoped would one day become family. "Rina, my girl! What are you doing in Jerusalem? It's not the Day of Atonement yet, is it? It's not Passover."

"My mother and I are hiding here. I don't know if you've heard."

"I'm afraid I know very little. How's my friend Hadwin?"

Rina couldn't find the words to answer.

"I see. Well, you and your mother are welcome to stay with us as long as you need. We have a little property on the other side of the garden of olives. We have plenty of food. You needn't concern yourself with being a street vendor. It isn't safe for a girl of your beauty."

"Thank you," Rina said softly. "You are very kind."

"I can help you here if you like."

"Yes, that would be—" The lump in her throat choked her words.

"Say no more. I'll be back with my wife, and she'll help you load your belongings onto my donkey. We can move you in today."

Rina could only nod by this point. She felt fortunate to have run into Elyam. Her mother was overjoyed when she heard the news. They knew no one in Jerusalem, and now there were friends whom they considered family.

CHAPTER 20

The way home seemed daunting to Ezekiel. The men decided to go into Chorazin to see if they could get supplies and fill their bellies before the trek home to Tiberias. Without a seaworthy vessel, the walk would be the better part of the day. Ezekiel decided to inspect the damage to the boat to see if repairs could be made.

But there was nothing left of it except some wooden planks that had washed onto shore overnight. They would have to walk, or he would find someone who had a vessel for sale. Without any currency on him, it would certainly be a test for his bartering skills.

His crew met him on the outskirts of town, returning with a few loaves that appeared surprisingly fresh.

"How did you buy these?"

"My family's from here, remember?" Youssef tossed him a loaf. "My brother and his wife have a market stand just inside the city. He said you can pay him later."

Ezekiel grinned. "It seems fortune has smiled upon us once again."

"It's God, not fortune," Youssef corrected.

Ezekiel didn't respond. Instead, he bit off a huge chunk of his loaf, chewing as fast as he could.

"I guess we should get started on the journey home," Youssef filled the silence. "It's going to take some time, but we're alive. That's what matters."

When his home came into view, Ezekiel broke into a run. Outside, he saw two Roman centurion horses. It was apparent his homecoming wouldn't be a joyous one. Once he reached the hut, he spied the silhouette of a man in chains accompanied by two soldiers. His eyes adjusted to the dim light as he caught his breath. At length, he mustered up the courage to ask what was going on.

The man in chains was almost unrecognizable until he spoke. "They have come for the dagger."

It was his father. Anger raged within him but was cooled only by concern for himself and his mother.

"I told these soldiers we do not know this man." His mother eyed him as if to say, follow along.

"Yes, this man began to follow me last week in the market. I think he's possessed."

"So, you do not know him?" barked the more prominent soldier.

"Of course not."

The other soldier paused to study their faces. Ezekiel froze. After what seemed like an eternity, he said, "See, I win the bet. This man's lying to us."

"Then why would Abigail say it was here?"

"Who knows? She is a cunning woman and maybe she wanted us to punish this family for something."

"I don't know. It doesn't seem right to me."

"Okay we should kill them anyway."

"No! We would have a village uprising if we did. No! we will let them be for now."

"Okay . . . C'mon!" said the soldier yanking on the lead chain. Dismas lurched to his feet.

Unconvinced, the larger soldier reached into his satchel, pulled out a pile of coins, and handed them to his partner.

"We looked everywhere. No sign of the dagger," the smaller one said, counting the coins smugly.

"I still don't like it. These Hebrews are known liars."

"Please. We're not lying. My father was killed eight years ago, fighting in Germania. He defected from the Hebrew faith. We have to live with the shame of his infidelity to God and are just trying to make up for it."

"Well, you don't smell like someone who has come into money," the large soldier quipped, making the smaller laugh out loud. In one swift motion, they grabbed Dismas and pulled him outside. Making him walk at the end of the chain was part of the humiliation.

Aaliyah held back tears until it was safe. Ezekiel didn't say anything. He didn't have to. The sheer terror on his mother's face said everything. They just stood there, each trying to process what had just happened.

Ezekiel waited until the next day to go to the market. He let his fisherman have the day off with pay this time. They certainly earned it. *I am just relieved we were not having a funeral for any of them,* he thought. He made his way to Eliab's stand.

"How are you doing my young friend?" asked Eliab.

"I need to buy the dagger back."

"You mean the dagger that you sold me? It has been quite some time. I sold it already."

"To who?"

"To a rich young lady. I have to say she was quite pretty. Why do you need it back?"

"That's my business."

"Well she asked where it came from as well. She threatened me and my family. It's obvious she is a Roman citizen."

Ezekiel grabbed him by the cloak. "Tell me you didn't tell her who sold it to you?"

"I uh . . ." Ezekiel slammed him up against the wall.

"I couldn't help it! I found out it was stolen and I would have lost everything. She paid me well for it." Ezekiel pushed off of the old man. He knew the kind of family Abigail came from.

"You have just cursed my family!"

Ezekiel turned. Heat emanated from under his cloak as his anger burned. *I have to get this dagger back,* he thought. *Everyone has a price.*

CHAPTER 21

Elyam made the arrangements with Ester and Rina. They would live with him and Bathshua. He was willing to claim Rina as his granddaughter, so no one would think there was any impropriety.

The preparations for the move took only half a day. They made quick work of the tent and all their belongings. He knew Bathshua was grateful for the help. Rina and her mother were hard workers, making Bathshua's life easier since she was getting on in years.

Elyam did his best to talk up the fact that his "granddaughter" was living with them. He even made up an elaborate story as to why she wasn't married at her age. Each evening he practiced the story with Rina, so it would ring true if anyone asked. It would look bad before the Sanhedrin otherwise.

On this night, after he practiced the lie with Rina, he went to his room, said his prayers, and retired for the evening. He looked at the ceiling, his forehead creased with worry about Aaliyah and Ezekiel. He hadn't heard from them in a while.

Bathshua, came to his room and blew out the oil lamp. "I've seen that look before."

"I can't help it. I keep worrying about them. I think it might be time for me to take a trip to Tiberias."

"I would go with you, but it would leave our guests alone."

"My dear, if you went with me, I would feel like a king showing off my queen to a foreign land."

"Oh, stop it! I'm far from a queen. Just hold me for a little while. I'll make preparations for your journey in the morning."

"I don't know what I did to deserve a woman so elegant."

"You are a lying old fool. But I like the lies you tell."

"It's how I keep you interested."

"It's certainly never boring with you, Elyam."

"My dear Bathshua, you have a way to put me at ease even when my soul is troubled."

She cuddled even more and fell asleep but rest eluded Elyam. He began to shiver. Carefully, he pulled his arm from underneath his wife and stoked the embers in the clay stove nearby.

"God, please be with Ezekiel! He's becoming a fine man, but I fear he's falling away from you. Help him, please. He needs you now more than ever."

A wind blew through the house at that moment and extinguished the embers of the fire. Elyam spent the rest of the night praying.

The next morning, he felt weary. He didn't relish the long trip ahead. He waved goodbye to the women and left for his journey. His donkey was weighed down with gifts and provisions of dried lamb meat, wine, and grain.

He made it to midday before the effects of the sleepless night caught up with him. He found a shady spot behind a large boulder with a tree where he could tie up his donkey. No sooner had he done this when sleep overcame him.

Elyam walked among a garden of olive trees. Each tree was alive, with branches twisting into dreadful shapes. Each one became a Roman cross.

When he looked back, he saw all his loved ones hanging from them. He tried to run, but each cross had a Roman soldier blocking his way. He tried to scream, but his mouth wouldn't open.

The circle of soldiers closed around him until he was unable to move. Elyam looked at his hands, and they were covered in blood. He looked up, and a column of fire descended from the heavens, consuming the crosses. Suddenly, his face felt like a warm cloth was wiping it from chin to forehead.

He woke, looking into the face of the donkey. The animal was about to lick his face a second time.

"Get off of me, you wretched beast!" Elyam sat up and let his eyes adjust to his surroundings. The sun was setting, displaying a fiery tapestry across the sky.

"I should get moving," he said to the donkey. Even though his dream plagued him, the rest had helped somewhat. He walked through the night using an oil lamp. Fear kept him alert.

The new-moon sky was clear that night. The stars seemed so close you could touch them. But the light they provided wasn't enough for Elyam's tired eyes. His mind saw things that weren't there. He jumped each time a branch swayed in the wind.

"I don't know how many more times I can make this trip," he said aloud, prompting a bray from his donkey.

"It's alright. We'll be there soon. If I know my daughter, she will be overjoyed to see us. I just hope they're okay."

Just then, a stench came upon them—a stench so strong it could have knocked him over if he weren't expecting it. It was the dreaded stench of crucified prisoners. Their corpses were left to rot as a warning to others. The Romans didn't crucify often, but they liked to leave the bodies up for weeks when they did.

He could see the bodies silhouetted against the stars. Some were only halfway on the crosses. The fear of crucifixion affected the community. Only the Zealots dared to defy the Romans. Most wanted peace, but the Zealots were making things harder for everyone else.

CHAPTER 22

Hadwin wandered through the Highlands region of Galilee just north of the Jezreel valley. The night he fled, he had been able to get more provisions from his house before moving to this region, a known hideout of the Zealots.

As he walked along, he came upon an encampment where several men were roasting a goat on a spit. The smell of the fresh meat was welcome to his starving belly. He hid in the shadows until sundown when the men were having their fill of wine and meat.

It wasn't long before each of the drunkards fell asleep by the fire. Once he saw the last one drift away, he quietly crept to the half-eaten goat. He pulled off chunks of meat, wrapped them in a cloth, and slipped into the night.

He kept walking until he had made his way to a stream.

He unwrapped his meal and dug in. Without any wine to wash down the meat, he felt as though he might choke. Kneeling beside the stream, he cupped a mouthful of water in his hands. But no sooner had the water slid down his throat did he feel the sharp edge of a sword at his neck.

"You thought you could steal our food without being noticed?"

Hadwin slowly stood up. "If you're going to kill me, please do it quickly."

"Who are you?"

"My name is Hadwin. People think I'm dead. I wish you no harm. I'm just starving and needed food. I'm willing to work for it."

"I'm going to back up now. Turn around slowly, so I can see your face."

Hadwin turned as the flicker of a torch lit the faces of three men, all with swords drawn.

"As you can see, I have no weapons. If I wished harm on you, I would be heavily armed."

"If you had asked, we would have freely given you a meal. We are Hebrews, after all."

"I don't know who a friend or enemy is anymore," Hadwin responded.

The leader of the group lowered his sword and motioned for the others to do the same. They smelled of sweat and cheap wine.

"Well, you are either running from the Romans, or you're a thief. Either way, we can accommodate you." The men spat on the ground at the word Roman. Hadwin smiled. At least he knew where these men stood when it came to the Romans.

Back at their camp, he told them his story. All three listened intently. Hadwin left out the part about Yeshua and Luke by merely saying his injury was not life-threatening. As the wine dwindled, they fell asleep one by one.

The next morning, Hadwin helped the men by fixing some food. As they ate, he noticed they kept watch.

"I've told you my story. Now tell me yours."

"We're Zealots," said Markeus, the leader. "We were overtaken by a band of Roman sympathizers. They ran their horses through our midst. All of us were able to move out of the way, except for Simeon. He's in that tent over there. He cannot walk. We want to go see this Yeshua people speak of. Some say he has the power to heal the lame."

"I've met this Yeshua and can attest to his healing power."

"Well, I still say this is a fool's errand," Benjamin, the youngest of their group, said.

Hadwin admired the faith of this group. "I left something out of my story. I almost died from the sword wound. Yeshua came to where I was and healed me. I think he's a friend of a physician there named Luke. "

"Then let's go and find him. Did you say this happened in Tiberias?"

"Yes, however, I cannot go back there. The family of Asher thinks I'm dead. They cannot know I'm alive, or they'll hunt my family down."

"Then we'll part ways in Nazareth. Surely you won't be hunted there. That is, unless you have somewhere important you have to go?"

"No, not in particular. I know you need help with Simeon. I'll go as far as Nazareth."

"Good!" said Markeus.

Hadwin felt fortunate to have met this group. They evidently loved their comrade, and that kind of devotion couldn't come from evil hearts. As they made their way to Nazareth, the men told jokes to ease Simeon's pain. The going was slow and methodical. People handed them coins as they passed, which encouraged the men as they moved along. Hadwin relished the company. Losing his family felt like losing his soul.

Upon reaching Nazareth, they asked about Rabbi Yeshua, but no one seemed to know where the son of Joseph had gone. Some of the people in the market suggested he and his followers were headed for Capernaum. Still, it was a long journey to go on with only a hunch.

At the synagogue, one of the priests confirmed he saw a rabbi fitting Yeshua's description with a band of followers headed in the direction of Capernaum. It was now midday. The men decided to press on.

The trip would take them two days, and their friend was getting worse.

Simeon had developed a fever and slipped into a deep sleep. They needed to find Yeshua soon. Hadwin carried the front of the platform which held Simeon. Though he was old, he seemed to relish the task, if only to show the younger men he still had what it took.

It was sundown on the second day of their journey when they reached Capernaum. The men, utterly exhausted, pitched a tent on the outskirts of the city. They sent Hadwin into town to decipher the whereabouts of Yeshua and his disciples.

"Excuse me. Excuse me," he said to a young man who was carrying grain. "Do you know of this man called Yeshua?"

"There are many Yeshua's in Galilee. I think they all migrated from Jerusalem. If you're referring to the rabbi who claims to be the Messiah, he'll be teaching in the morning at the house of Matthew, the tax collector."

"Do you know where he lives?"

"No, I can't be bothered with the whereabouts of a tax collector. As far as I'm concerned, no self-respecting Hebrew would go near the place."

"Thank you for your time."

"Shalom."

Hadwin returned to camp. It was a perfect spot beside a small stream. All the men had to eat was bread, but the water was a welcome sight. Simeon had spiked a fever, which worried Hadwin.

He had seen this before. When someone was injured in the vineyard, if a fever ensued, it meant death wasn't far behind. He kept this sentiment to himself, for there was nothing he could do besides wet one of his garments and lay it over Simeon's forehead.

"You seem to have the knowledge of a physician," said Markeus.

"The men in my charge at the vineyard looked to me when there was an accident. We need to see Yeshua soon."

Markeus nodded in agreement. The rest of the night was spent in silence. Each of the men stoked the hypnotic flames of their campfire.

CHAPTER 23

Abigail wanted to feel something other than rage. When she learned Hadwin was still alive, she ordered her servants to stone Jeremiah to death. It was a sickening thrill to watch the life drain from his face.

A feeling of power came with having the servants stone their comrade. All were afraid for their families' lives if they disobeyed.

She left his corpse by the side of the road. The remaining servants were forced to take an oath under the Hebrew God to never speak of the event.

As she settled back at home, she relished the feeling of revenge against men. It was men who made her this way. It was men who abused her. It was men who treated her like property. Now she needed a plan. She needed to find Ezekiel's family. She would make them pay. They must know where Hadwin was.

She had everything taken from the house that reminded her of her brother and father. Each statue was defaced and crumbled. Abigail saw to it that each one was removed and buried in a rubble heap behind the house. The mead coffers were drained and turned back into wine storage. The Hebrews didn't go for the strong-tasting liquid. They loved their traditions as much as their ridiculous holidays. She had enough money to live the rest of her days in luxury, but that didn't appease the torture in her soul. She needed revenge. With a goblet of wine in one hand, she reclined on her Roman dining couch. Her sandals were killing her feet, so they came off.

She dismissed her servants to be alone.

She needed companionship, but not the commitment of being someone's wife. In the morning, she would find a good-looking servant to fill her needs. Ezekiel would not do. He smelled of fish all the time, and he had too much integrity to be a manservant. No, he hadn't taken the bait of the dagger.

She would just have to hold onto it and wait. Let guilt enter Ezekiel's mind until he was ready to save his father's life. She needed him to fill her need to punish all men. He was good. Too good. Men like that appealed to her compassion then took advantage of her.

Strangely, she was attracted to him. Her rage needed a target. And for that, Ezekiel would do nicely.

CHAPTER 24

E lyam was glad to have passed the crucifixions. The air smelled
cleaner as he neared the center of Tiberias. Even the fish market
was better than the stench of rotting human flesh. At one of the stands,
he bought some cheese and pickled sardines—a welcomed meal after
such a long journey. It was strange to return to the place he once called
home. Nostalgia would have been more potent had it not been for the
nature of his visit.

The Sea of Galilee was peaceful in the late morning hours. Fishermen
were casting nets and pulling in the tilapia and freshwater sardines. It
was different here. The work was difficult, but life seemed to move at
a slower pace than in Jerusalem. As he neared his daughter's house, he
tried to make himself more presentable. Aaliyah ran out to greet him.

"Abba! You came to see us." She hugged her father.

"Yes, my child, I did. And I brought gifts. Where's my favorite
grandson?"

"At the moment, I don't know. But I'm sure he'll be home soon. Please come inside. I have so much to tell you."

"I heard about Hadwin."

"Yes, us too. I'm worried about Ester and Rina. We don't know where they went."

"Then I have some good news for you. They're with Bathshua in Jerusalem. They're safe."

"Is it true Hadwin killed Asher?"

"If so, then he'll bring shame to his family."

"I don't know if that's true. Hadwin was a good man and wouldn't harm someone without good reason. May God have mercy on his soul."

"Is Ezekiel taking good care of you?"

"Yes, he is. But I fear he's losing faith in Yahweh. He hints at disbelief and the way of the Sadducees."

"He's been through a lot. Enough for two lifetimes."

"Well, I'm sure he'll be home soon. Lay down and get some sleep. I'll get the basin for you to wash up first."

Elyam wasn't used to sleeping during the day, but it wasn't long before the heaviness of his eyelids took over. When he woke, the sun painted the sky with red and orange. Outside the house, Ezekiel was staring out over the water.

"Ezekiel!"

He turned to face his grandfather. "Saba!" Ezekiel hugged him so hard it almost took Elyam's breath from his lungs. "How's everything in Jerusalem?"

"Busy! Your grandmother keeps me working harder than ever."

"I don't think it's her."

"I have to blame it on someone." Elyam smiled at the sentiment.

"You haven't changed."

"When you're this handsome and intelligent, why change?"

"We've been worried about you."

"You, my dear Ezekiel, are not to worry. That's your grandmother's job. I think she worries enough for the entire family. I know someone else who worries a lot about you—your friend Rina."

"Have you heard from them? We have no idea where they went."

"They're secretly living with us in Jerusalem. You know, Zeke, you might want to take her as your wife now."

"I don't think she would have me."

"She loves you, Zeke. She was forced into an engagement with Asher. You could restore her honor."

"Is that why you made this trip? To convince me to marry?"

"No! We were all worried."

"As you should be," interrupted Aaliyah.

"When we hadn't heard from you in a while, I decided to come back and make sure you and your mother were well."

"We are."

"No, we're not!" exclaimed Aaliyah. "Hadwin was murdered, Roman soldiers came looking for a dagger with your father in chains, and you say we are well?"

"What's this business with Roman soldiers?"

"It's nothing, really. My father gave me something to keep for him years ago. Now it's lost, and they took him away. I mean, hey, I thought he was dead anyway."

Elyam studied his grandson's face. He could see it was a lie, but wisdom told him not to push the issue any further. "And how is your business going?"

"I'm down to one boat and crew. I was planning on building four more."

"Don't you have enough to live on for the time being?"

"I like the work."

"Is that why you're at home when your crew is out fishing?"

"I had some business to attend to."

"You're not a good liar, my boy."

"Well, we had a shipwreck a few days ago, and I guess I haven't been myself since."

"See, now we're getting somewhere. You know, I say a prayer for you and your mother daily."

"Thank you."

They stood in silence for the next few seconds, trying to ascertain the truth from one another.

"Do you think Rina would want to see me?"

"I know she would. Why don't you and your mother come to Jerusalem?"

"I don't think we could. I'd have to leave my business."

"Rina cannot come here. Surely you know that. The only chance you have with her is to move there."

"Saba, I've already closed my heart off to that possibility. She was the reason I went into business in the first place."

"Then she is as good of a reason to go out of business. You have one lifetime and one lifetime only to share with the woman you love."

"You sound like a rabbi."

"Well, Bathshua always said I missed my purpose in life."

"Abba, you should take us back with you," said Aaliyah.

"If you want to go with him, I can run things here and be in Jerusalem before Sabbath each week."

"And who would cook for you and make sure you had the strength to keep fishing?"

"I can take care of myself, Mother. You should go with Elyam. If I were to come, I would have to sell my boat first and make sure my crew has employment."

"We can talk about all of this in the morning. For now, I'm preparing a meal. Let's talk of lighter things for the rest of the evening."

Aaliyah made an exquisite meal of dates, fish, and lamb stew. Ezekiel thought it tasted heavenly. It was good to see his grandfather. It was good to hear news about Rina and Ester. He had imagined the worst since hearing of their disappearance. Maybe it was time for him to think about Rina once more.

Her independent spirit and friendship had meant more to him than anything in the world. It felt like a betrayal when she allowed herself to be betrothed. He knew she didn't have a choice at the time, but his heart still ached at the memory. He never wanted to be hurt like that again.

As he lay on his mat, he dreamed about what it might be like to marry her. When she was around, he always had a friend. He wondered, though, if her father's death had changed her. The night seemed lighter now. He drifted into a sleep far more peaceful than he had experienced in the recent past.

Lately, his dreams had turned into nightmares since disowning his father before the Roman soldiers. A part of him felt guilty, but another part wanted Dismas to suffer for abandoning and shaming the family. The main reason he couldn't go back to Jerusalem with Elyam was that the dagger issue still wasn't settled. *I might be able to free my father if I return it,* he thought. It might do him some good to have his mother in Jerusalem instead of in Tiberias.

CHAPTER 25

Hadwin struggled to keep pace with the other Zealots. It was his turn to carry Simeon on the wheeled cart. Trying to be gentle but quick, He moved along with his companions toward Matthew's house.

People were crowded outside. Try as they might, they couldn't get through.

"Excuse us, we have a sick man here! Please let us through!" exclaimed Markeus.

"We all have sick loved ones. Wait your turn! This is the last hope anyway!" shouted one man who propped up his young son.

"I have an idea!" said Hadwin. "Look! The houses are close together. If we can get him on the roof, we can move him over there. Then we can lower him through."

"I don't know."

"It's our only chance!"

They carried Simeon down the street, picked him up, and put him on his stretcher. Then the men attached their ropes to each of the poles and tied Simeon to the structure.

"Alright. Markeus and I will crawl up to the roof."

The men hoisted Simeon to the roof. Then, carefully, they walked the beams from house to house until they were directly over the tax collector's home. Reeds made up a covering in the middle of the structure, so they pulled them away to uncover the opening. They heard gasps from inside. Some of the people below began to curse.

They could see Yeshua looking up at them as they lowered Simeon into the crowd.

"Friend, your sins are forgiven," he said.

Several religious leaders appeared affronted by this, but whatever they were thinking, they kept it to themselves.

"Why are you thinking these things in your hearts?" Yeshua turned to them.

The men were stunned.

"Which is easier to say, 'your sins are forgiven,' or, 'get up and walk?' But I want you to know that the Son of Man has authority on earth to forgive sins." Yeshua looked at Simeon. "I say to you, get up, take your mat, and go home."

Simeon looked around, somewhat dazed. Hadwin couldn't believe his eyes. This man was on death's door and now looked healthy. He rolled up his mat and grinned with delight. Yeshua's gaze turned to Hadwin. They exchanged smiles.

The crowd grew alive with excitement. It was the first time many of them had seen a miracle of this magnitude. But Hadwin's joy halted when he recognized several faces in the crowd. Some of the men present had worked for him in Tiberias. Because of the excitement, he managed to slip away unnoticed by all except Markeus.

He decided the only way to keep his family safe was to travel to Kush. The Kushite people were known to be hospitable, and he could possibly make a new life there. He walked along the Sea of Galilee on the northern bank. Going south, he would have to travel through Jerusalem toward Egypt. Maybe he could find Ester and Rina while passing through, just to let them know he was alive.

He looked unkempt, for it had been many days since he had bathed properly. His beard had grown to an unruly length. But he now had a full belly and enough energy to keep moving at a good pace. He would have to evade capture along the way, but his poor appearance acted as a sort of disguise. After all, the men who had worked for him knew him to be fastidious about his personal grooming. His gray curly hair was now pulled back over his shoulders. He let the locks cascade in front of his face as he walked. If his appearance didn't keep people away, his smell definitely would.

I could clean up in Jerusalem before making the trek to Kush, he thought. The desire to see his family was overwhelming. With each step, his legs felt heavier, but he had to keep on. He had to keep moving.

CHAPTER 26

"Go find Hadwin," Abigail ordered her head servant. "He has to be in the surrounding area. Take each servant who knows what he looks like and send them in pairs to each town."

"You know what you're asking, right? Many of these men have worked for him. They respect him. How do you know they won't just say they didn't see him?"

"We threaten their families. They've already seen what we can do. They will sell him out if they find him."

"As you wish."

"And another thing. You might try going to Jerusalem. All Hebrews like to be close to the Temple."

Her servant nodded and left.

She sat down to make a plan. Now that her servants were out looking for Hadwin, she would have to do much of her own housework. It would be good to do some manual labor for a change. She hadn't done any since a previous marriage. Neither one wanted to wed the other, but Asher had arranged the match to solidify a contract with a wealthy winemaker in Nazareth.

Maybe she could go to Samaria and live in one of their houses until her servants found Hadwin. She would take a servant with her to pose as her husband to avoid suspicion. He should be a handsome man who looked as though he deserved someone like her. Then it was settled. Her first order of business would be to find such a man.

She found the suitor in a well-muscled servant named Cassius. He looked the part. Dark curly hair with unnatural blue eyes that sparkled with every smile. For a servant, his personal grooming was impeccable. Abigail was going to enjoy this. Cassius had no immediate family and no reason to say no. Like her, he was an opportunist. As he packed his satchel, Abigail watched in a lustful gaze.

The road to Sychar in the region of Samaria was quiet except for the merchants who were in a hurry to get into the city without notice. Many of them were Hebrew, and it would bring shame on their families if they were known to associate with the half-breeds.

Abigail kept her face covering on to hide the nature of her visit until the right time.

Apart from the Temple of Nergal and the Temple of Mount Gerizim, where the Samaritans worshiped Yahweh, it looked like all the other cities in the region. Abigail remembered her grandfather teaching her the Samaritan beliefs and how the Temple of Mount Gerizim was the true place to worship Yahweh. She had always resented the two religions for their strict rules and hatred of one another.

Judaic symbols were carved into the stone of the temple. Hebrews walked on one side of the street, Samaritans on the other. The merchants sold meat, grapes, dates, and grain as well as textiles and weapons. The Romans had also built temples here. Among them stood the impressive Temple of Augustus—Herod's attempt to win favor with Rome.

This is a perfect place to hide out, thought Abigail, as she and her "husband" procured a dwelling where she could unwind. First, she would go to a well and bring in some water for her horses. It would look strange for her "husband" to go, so she gathered her clay jars and headed for the community well.

Most people seemed to have already retrieved their water for the day, as the well was deserted apart from one man who sat relaxing on a log.

She tried to go about her task without making eye contact.

"Hello. Will you give me a drink?" asked the strange man.

"How can you, a Jew, ask me, a Samaritan woman, for a drink?"

"If you knew who it was that asks you for a drink, you would have asked him, and he would have given you living water."

"I can see you have no jars, and the well is deep. How can you get this 'living water?' Do you think you're better than our ancestor Jacob, who dug this well?"

"Everyone who drinks the water from this well will be thirsty again, but those who drink the water I give them will never thirst again."

"Sir, give me this water. I don't want to have to fetch water from this well again."

"Why don't you call your husband and come back?"

"I don't have a husband." Abigail knew she couldn't fake the servitude of a married woman at this point.

"You're right. The man you're living with now isn't your husband, but you've been married five times."

After a moment of silence, Abigail could barely utter, "That's true."

She felt undressed before this man, as if every thought she'd ever had was suddenly exposed. She needed to gain a foothold again. Her mind flailed for a response. "I can see you're a prophet. Our ancestors worshipped on this mountain, but you Jews say we must worship in Jerusalem."

"One day you will neither worship Yahweh on this mountain or in Jerusalem. You don't know who you worship. Even though salvation has come from the Jews, true worshippers can worship the Father in spirit and in truth. Do you know what truth is?"

Again, he disarmed her. She felt the pit of her stomach churn as though she had swallowed a live fish.

"I know a Messiah is supposed to come and explain all these things to us."

"I am the one."

This can't be true, Abigail thought to herself. She struggled with what had just happened. She still had to keep a low profile, but she couldn't hold in the feelings that welled up inside of her. It felt like a war within her spirit.

After noticing more men coming down the path, she gathered her things and set off toward town, where Cassius was waiting for her return.

"There's nothing in these jars!" He exclaimed.

"Well, you don't know what just happened. There was a man in town who told me everything I ever did and claimed to be the Messiah!"

"The Messiah? That's just a myth."

"You weren't there! We have to leave soon. And you're going back to being my servant."

It was just as well. Cassius knew if they continued with this charade, Abigail would eventually have him killed or have to marry him to keep the Sanhedrin from finding out about their arrangement.

"I have to tell people in town about this man. It'll put the attention on him as we move on."

"Do you realize how crazy this sounds?"

Abigail checked her spirit. Something she hadn't felt in a long time plagued her—guilt. Deep down, she knew she would have to face her sins. She knew the man at the well understood the depths of her depravity. Her sins were exposed, and for once, she hated the ugliness of it all.

Removing her face covering, she walked onto the street below. "There's a man at the well of Jacob who told me everything I ever did. He could be the Messiah!"

People all around took notice. Some went to check out her claim while others stood there puzzled as to why a Samaritan woman would be this bold.

CHAPTER 27

E zekiel sold his remaining boat to a former employee. He didn't receive much, but it was enough to try buying back the dagger. While at the market, he purchased a sword. Knowing Abigail could have him killed at any moment didn't sit well with him. He hid it under his cloak as he approached her estate. The head servant came out to greet him.

"You need to leave," her head servant barked at the door. "Abigail isn't here!"

"But I need to talk to her."

"She's traveling, and no one knows when she'll return."

"Why is she traveling?"

The man ignored his question. "You must go and never return. Trust me—it's not safe for you here."

"You don't understand. She has something of mine that I need to buy back."

"Just leave and hurry."

Walking away, Ezekiel was grateful his mother had already left with Elyam. She, at least, was safe. He acknowledged to himself it could all be for nothing. His father might already be dead.

Now there was nothing holding him in Galilee, just a little land and a small dwelling where he had lived since birth. He wondered if he would ever return. Most likely not. Here, he was still the son of a thief. In Jerusalem, he could be anything he wanted.

He packed his things and set them beside the small donkey his mother had left behind, but he would wait until the next day to make the journey. He wanted one last night with his memories in this place.

With the morning sun came the inevitable dread of the journey. The journey itself wasn't difficult, but the thought of what he would say to Rina. He willed himself to get up. As he left town, he spotted Abigail's estate on the hill. Now that enough time had passed, he hated himself for denying his father, for sacrificing him to the Roman soldiers.

Tears welled in his eyes. He would try to save him now, if possible. Tying his donkey to a sycamore tree, he sat down and cried like he hadn't cried in a long time. People passing by seemed to avoid him, but it was just as well.

He sat there for about an hour when he noticed a man leading a donkey with a woman on it. As they grew closer, the pit of his stomach churned. It was Abigail. Mustering all his courage, he stood up to meet her. Beneath her face covering were tears.

"What brings you here, Ezekiel?"

"I need to purchase the dagger you bought in the market."

"I thought so. What's the dagger worth to you, the son of a thief?"

"It's just very important to me."

"The question is, *why* is it so important to you?"

"Because my father stole the dagger a long time ago, and I need to return it."

"You think you can buy back your father's life with this?" Her voice wavered. She produced the dagger which had been tucked in her waistband.

"I need to try."

"If you see Hadwin, tell him I need to see him. I won't harm him or have him imprisoned."

"Hadwin's alive?"

"I believe so, yes. Once Hadwin has met with me, you can have your dagger. No sooner."

"But I have money."

"I don't need or want your money. I need to talk to Hadwin. Deal?"

"Do I have a choice? What if he *is* dead?"

"He isn't. Believe me; he's alive and on the run."

"How do I know you won't kill him?"

"You have my word as a Roman and a Hebrew."

"I've known both to lie."

"Then you won't get your precious dagger." Lifting her chin, she dismounted the donkey.

Ezekiel backed up, his hand gripping the handle of the sword under his cloak.

"Don't worry; I'm not going to hurt you." She led the donkey away with Cassius close behind.

Ezekiel stood there, dumbfounded until his donkey's bray brought him back to the present.

The road to Jerusalem stank of rotting flesh. Looking up, Ezekiel realized the Romans had left a row of recent crosses up. As harrowing as the sight was, he needed to see if his father was among them. He wasn't, which brought an element of relief, but Ezekiel could no longer contain the contents of his stomach as the smell overwhelmed him.

He knew, if executed, his father would be among the worst offenders. There would be no room for mercy, no possibility of burying him according to Hebrew customs. He hated the Romans for their cruelty but understood why they used this method of execution. It kept the people fearful.

Clouds filled the sky, and he knew the rain would soon be upon him. At the first few drops, he secretly hoped it would come down in torrents, but all he got was a splattering of rain, which just made him miserable. His wineskin at least provided a small amount of relief. With each mile, he rewarded himself with a sip of wine.

The journey was more arduous than he remembered. As the day waned, he could see the light of torches in the city. In Tiberias, the town went to sleep at sundown, but here, it seemed alive late into the night.

As he approached the city center, he became aware of his sweaty stench. A night camped outside the city, and a swim in the Kishon river would do him good. With his donkey securely tied, he walked down to the riverbank by the light of an oil lamp. The water was cool against his skin.

He hung his clothes on a tree branch to dry and stepped back into the water. Floating on his back, he stared up at the night sky. The stars seemed to have a life of their own. How could one God create all of this? It took armies of slaves to build Rome.

Elyam would scold me for even thinking this.

As he drifted in the water, so did his thoughts. He felt something new—disconnection. He knew no one in Jerusalem except for family, and even then, he wasn't sure they would accept him if he couldn't provide. His thoughts turned to Rina.

How could she love him now? They had been apart for too long. Would she be the same? Asher wasn't honorable, and he could've taken her innocence without thinking twice to serve his own interest. Was she still a virgin? It would only matter if he believed in the old laws of

Moses, which he didn't. But somehow, it still mattered. These feelings only made him feel more disconnected.

Ezekiel gathered some wood and made a small fire. He laid out his clothes on a large, flat rock to dry. The flames created waves of orange light rolling off and disappearing into the sky. The sparks and smoke floated up, hypnotizing him until he fell asleep.

CHAPTER 28

The sunlight bled through Ezekiel's eyelids, waking him with a start the following morning. He quickly realized the privacy the darkness had afforded him was gone with the rising sun. Grabbing his cloaks, he jumped behind a tree and donned his tunic.

Lifting his sword, he tested its weight in his hand. It seemed well-balanced. He had never used a sword in his life, so, facing the tree, he thrust the blade into its trunk. It took some force to remove it. He tried a new method, swinging the blade downward in a chopping motion. The sword bounced off the tree, smacking him in the face. Embarrassed, he looked around to see if anyone was watching.

Off in the distance was a group of men coming up the path. He could hear them laughing. Surely, they hadn't witnessed his foolish mistake from that far? He hid the sword in his cloak. As the men drew closer, he felt beads of sweat on his forehead. Wiping his brow, his hand came back red. He leaned down beside the river to wash his face. Crimson drops dissipated in the water as the men approached.

He looked up, and the four men just stood there smiling. One of them, clearly the leader, folded his arms and said, "It looks like you had a fight with yourself and lost."

The rest snickered as Ezekiel's face turned red. Touching his forehead, he felt a gash and a bump. "I've never wielded a sword before. I decided to try a blow against that branch."

"First, you're holding it all wrong. Try this." He reached for the sword buried in Ezekiel's cloak. Ezekiel let the man have it.

Swinging the sword in an effortless motion, he said, "See? If you grip the sword like this, you have more control."

Ezekiel marveled at the skill the man demonstrated. "What's your name, sir?"

"I'm Sittish. I come from the Hittite country. You must excuse me and my men. It's been some time since we had such a laugh."

"Can you teach me?"

"To what? Get yourself killed?" Sittish paused for a moment. "Out of curiosity, why do you want to learn?"

"It just seemed like a good idea . . . in case I need to defend myself."

"Well, the world is a dangerous place. Let me look at your weapon for a moment." Sittish went silent as he tested its weight. "It's not very balanced. I'm afraid if you're as unskilled as you say, it won't serve you well."

His men said something in a language Ezekiel didn't understand. They reluctantly bowed and went on while Sittish stayed behind.

"First, an axe is made for chopping a tree. A sword is not. When you wield a sword, you must think of it as an extension of your arm. When I hold my arm out, it doesn't go to the tip of my fingers but to the tip of the sword. If the blade is unbalanced, you have to build up the strength to wield it."

"How do I use it if I'm attacked by a Roman?"

"You don't. Just pray they have mercy on you." Sittish, still holding Ezekiel's sword, pulled out another one. Holding each, he moved fluidly, swinging both swords as if they were counterpoints to the same weapon. His movements were so skillful Ezekiel just watched, mesmerized.

"You see, when the weapons become extensions of your arms, you can use them any way you want." Sittish stopped an inch from Ezekiel's face. Impressed that he didn't flinch, Sittish lowered the weapons and bowed. Ezekiel clumsily bowed back.

"I can teach you for a few hours then I must be on my way."

For the rest of the day, Sittish worked with Ezekiel. With each drill, Ezekiel improved his skill and felt more confident he could hold up in a fight.

"You've been a wonderful student. Now I must go and become a student as well."

"Really? Who's to be your teacher?"

"I must go and find him. His name is Yeshua."

"I know him."

"You know the great teacher of the Jews and yet you don't want to follow him?"

"It's complicated." Ezekiel looked down.

"It always is, my friend. I want to learn all I can from teachers who have wisdom." Sittish picked up his cloaks and sword. "Good luck with your Romans. I hope you don't end up on one of their crosses."

CHAPTER 29

Rina looked around as she did her chores. Although much had changed, her life felt the same in many ways. As a woman, Jerusalem was stricter on her than Tiberias. The influence of the world on Tiberias allowed for women to own property. In Jerusalem, the Pharisees and Sanhedrin made sure the law of Moses was strictly enforced. She'd even heard one of the religious officials praying out loud in the market, stating how thankful he was not to be a woman or a Gentile.

What she was looking for she couldn't say. She just longed for a freedom she had never experienced. She longed to be seen as the treasure she was, not just "another silly girl," as many of the older folks were fond of saying. The only times she came close to that feeling were when she had worked with her father at the vineyard. He and Ezekiel were the only two who seemed to see beyond her gender to the person. Elyam did his best, but even he had preconceived ideas as to what a woman should be or do.

This made the news that Ezekiel wasn't returning with Elyam even more devastating. She felt abandoned. Again.

Rina knew she had no right to feel this way. She was the one who'd betrayed Ezekiel. She didn't blame him for never wanting to speak to her again. It was a wonder her mother didn't blame her for their misfortunes. They still didn't know if Hadwin was dead or alive, and the days just kept going by.

Today, all but Rina had gone into the market to sell some of Elyam's livestock. She stayed behind because it was her "time." The menfolk were commanded to stay away from women when they bled. It was only a few days, but it felt like each month she was being rejected.

Ezekiel had never treated her this way. She remembered him coming to the door only to have her mother shoo him away. She longed for her friend.

While tidying up, she decided to go for a walk. It was a nice day, and the walls of their hut were closing in on her. There were days when she hated being a woman. She hated even more the injustices she saw toward women like herself. The Roman women had more rights than she did.

No one was around, but still she covered her face and walked to a nearby garden. The garden was filled with olive trees, some of which looked very old. As the sun peeked through the trees, she remembered her father taking her through the vineyards as a little girl. Rina remembered how strong she thought her father was, and how she felt nothing bad could happen so long as he was around. Ezekiel possessed the same strength, but somehow, she resented it in him.

She remembered the lamb she had rescued and how that lamb was fattened to feed her family during a difficult time. Her attempt to help an animal still ended with its death.

CHAPTER 30

R ina enjoyed her day alone. Everything in her life seemed to revolve around other people—keeping her mother comfortable, laughing at Elyam's silly stories. All of it designed to please others. Nothing in her life was for herself. It was as if the whole world wished her to be a slave.

She was tired of people telling her how to act, think, and feel. She missed her childhood in Tiberias, when things were simpler. She could be friends with boys without inciting suspicion. A tear rolled down her cheek. She had never felt this frustrated or vulnerable before. She fought hard to keep more tears from following, but they flowed out like the sudden storms that rolled off the Sea of Galilee. She was thankful to be alone. Her mother would call her weak for showing this much emotion.

She neared the Temple Mount and noticed a crowd of people around a stone seat. Each synagogue had one. It was called the "Seat of Moses."

"Thank the God of Abraham if you were born a man and not a woman. For the woman is given to emotion and easily tricked. Be even more thankful if you were born a man of the tribe of Levi. For the knowledge of God is given to him. Do not look to the Samaritans for friendship, for they worship God on the wrong mountain."

With every word the teacher spoke, Rina grew angrier. Weren't women children of God as well? Was it not said the glory of a man is his wife? How could this Pharisee teach with such hateful language? Turning to leave, she heard him say, "And there goes one now who's no doubt offended by the truth!"

Laughter erupted from the crowd.

Rina just kept her head down and kept walking, determined not to let her emotions prove this horrible man right. She quickened her pace. The direction didn't matter as long as it was away. Once she passed the temple, the mood changed in the city. People went about their business amid the hustle and bustle of the markets. The more she walked, the better she felt. Getting out of the house felt like freeing her thoughts from a prison. The smell of bread baking in clay ovens even made her smile.

The sun was now in the middle of the sky. In the distance, however, she could see clouds forming. *I better get back.* She didn't want to go by the temple again, but it was the closest route home. Turning to leave, she noticed a man watching her from three houses away. The man bore a resemblance to her father. She told herself it couldn't be. She was imagining things. But she wanted to be sure. Hazarding a glance back, it was too late. The man had disappeared.

The clouds seemed to be gaining on her now as she neared the temple. The crowd had since dispersed, the seat of Moses, empty. It struck her as odd that the same seat was used to teach love and hate at the same time. She felt the first drops of rain. Now almost running, she could see their home not far ahead.

"Rina!"

She was in such a hurry to escape the rain she failed to notice the man approaching until they nearly collided. His voice knocked the wind out of her.

CHAPTER 31

"Rina!" Ezekiel helped her up. Together, they stood in the rain, their eyes locked in a gaze he had only dreamed about until now. But anger soon replaced shock in her beautiful eyes.

"I don't need your help!" Her response stung him. "How dare you come back now!"

"I'm happy to see you too."

"I'm sorry, but you have to leave."

"Why?"

"Because I'm unclean!"

"You know that never bothered me."

"Well, it bothers me!"

"So, you would leave me out in the rain?" Ezekiel noticed she wouldn't meet his eyes. "I'll stay on one side of the room, and you can stay on the other. I just want to talk."

"We have nothing to talk about."

"It seems like we have *a lot* to talk about."

"Look, I cannot hear another word about you not forgiving me, or how I was wrong for agreeing to marry Asher. I know—if I hadn't, my father would still be here!"

"I never said those things. If anything, this never would have happened if I hadn't punched Asher that night."

"You're right. It is your fault! If you had just minded your own business, none of this would have happened!"

"If it concerns you, then it's my business. All I ever wanted was to build a life for you! How do I get repaid? By watching you run off with that Roman! Even as your friend, I've always just wanted the best for you!"

"I don't need rescuing! I am not helpless!"

"Clearly! You know, maybe you're right. I should leave." Turning from her, he stormed off, completely drenched.

Since staying at Elyam's was not an option, Ezekiel powered through the rain to the outskirts of Jerusalem. He managed to find the tree where his donkey was still tethered, happily munching on damp hay. Fortunately, the rain had abated by now. Setting his sword against the tree, he turned to hang his clothes on a branch when he sensed someone behind him.

Spinning around, he met a hooded figure, who pointed the blade of his own sword at him.

"I can tell you're a fisherman and not a warrior." The man said in a familiar voice. Pulling back the hood, the man revealed himself.

"Hadwin? I thought you died! Abigail said you lived, but I didn't believe her." Ezekiel stepped into a hug, which seemed to take Hadwin by surprise.

"Well, I'm very much alive. I am curious, though. What were you speaking about with my daughter just now?"

"You were watching us?"

Hadwin nodded. "I've been living in the shadows for some time now. I came here hoping to spot Rina, and I did. I saw her in the street earlier today, but she doesn't know it was me. I followed her back to the house where you two were."

"It's Elyam's house. My mother is staying there, along with Ester and Rina. I came to visit, but everyone was away."

"Except for Rina."

"Yes. Except for her."

"Well, never leave your sword out of sight, my boy! That's how you get killed."

Ezekiel grinned sheepishly.

"Do you have any food?"

"A little. But it might be spoiled now from the rain."

"Do you think we can build a fire? I'm freezing."

"I think all the wood's wet too. However—" A thought came to him. He pulled a small flask of oil from his satchel. "Can I have my sword back?"

"Yes, here you go."

Ezekiel took a branch from the ground and used the sword to shave off the outer bark, exposing the dry heartwood fibers. He soaked some in oil and encased them with the remaining dry fibers. Placing them on a rock, he grabbed two stones and began striking them over the pile. With several strikes, the beginnings of an ember emerged, but it diminished as soon as it appeared.

A few more strikes, and Ezekiel gently blew on the pile. The pile burst into flames, allowing the men to add larger pieces of wood. It wasn't long before they had a raging fire. The success lifted their spirits. Both men laid on their backs, watching the embers rise to the heavens.

"Rina will be glad to know you're alive," Ezekiel said to break the silence.

"You can't tell her."

He knew why. "What do you want me to say?"

"Nothing. Talk about me as if I'm dead."

"Then why seek me out? Why let me know you're alive?"

"I figured someone needs to know, and I trust you."

"Why? I'm the son of a thief, after all."

"You're no more a thief than I'm a murderer. You're not responsible for the sins of your father."

"Not according to the Sanhedrin." Ezekiel looked into the fire, which was burning hotter now. His eyes became misty, and even in the dim firelight it was difficult to hide. "Abigail has a dagger my father stole. I need to get it back to spare his life. The only way she'll sell it to me is if you go to her. She believes you're alive."

"How could she know that?"

"I don't know. Maybe she visited your tomb. Are you willing to meet with her?"

"She'll kill me for sure."

"I have a plan."

"No. I cannot risk losing my life for a thief. No offense."

"I thought you said I wasn't a thief."

"You're not, but your father is. If he's still alive."

"Like I said, I have a plan."

"No!"

"Then what kind of life do you hope to have? Your family already thinks you're dead, so if she kills you, so what? You know Elyam and I will take care of Rina and Ester. But if this works and you live, then you'll have come back from the grave in their eyes. You have the chance to be a family again. Who knows, you might even get your own vineyard out of it."

Ezekiel could see Hadwin pondering the idea.

"All of your life, you've been a fighter. When I was little, I looked at you and wished you were my father. You were wise, loving, and you took care of your family. You deserve to see them again, and not as a fugitive."

The firelight bounced off a tear that ran down Hadwin's cheek. "Can I give you my answer in the morning?"

"Of course."

After a moment of silence, conversation picked back up again. But it wasn't long before both fell asleep to the sound of crackling flames.

CHAPTER 32

Rina was ashamed of herself. Never, in all her imaginings of meeting Ezekiel again, did she think she would react as she had. But the combination of her weighty thoughts and feelings and the shock of his sudden appearance proved more than she could take. The night had come, and with it, Elyam, Bathshua, Aaliyah, and Ester returned from the market.

Once more, the house was alive with preparations for the next day. Although separated from them, Rina could hear their voices in the next room. She decided not to tell them Ezekiel had come by. It was inappropriate for her to be with him unchaperoned. Especially in Jerusalem. She only hoped her reaction hadn't pushed him away for good. In her heart, she knew that wasn't the case. He would come back to her.

The next day, Rina woke to the sound of birds chirping. Unexpected happiness shone on her face in a way that was difficult to hide even with her face covering. Her mother looked at her with quizzical eyes. Elyam and Bathshua engaged in their usual banter while the morning grew in brightness.

As Aaliyah helped her with the morning preparations, Rina couldn't help but notice her downcast face. "What's wrong?"

"It's nothing."

"I have something to tell you a little bit later," she whispered. The thought of Ezekiel being in Jerusalem might cheer her up.

"Alright."

"What are you ladies talking about over there?" asked Elyam.

"Nothing! Nothing at all." Rina smiled under her face covering. For the meantime, it was nice to have a secret all her own.

CHAPTER 33

T he sun peeked above the olive trees and vineyards that scattered the countryside, waking Ezekiel and Hadwin slowly.

"We need to get moving," Ezekiel said behind a yawn.

"I never said I was willing to go along with this."

"Yes, you did."

"When?"

"When you stayed the night here instead of building your own camp elsewhere."

"Alright, I admit it. I'm interested in your plan. But I haven't made up my mind for certain yet."

"At any rate, let's go back to Tiberias. We can plan from there."

Hadwin agreed, and it wasn't long before they were on the road. The way through Nazareth seemed the safest route. Abigail's men weren't likely to find them there.

"You look suspicious." Ezekiel indicated his companion's hood. "Just walk in plain sight."

"What if someone recognizes me?"

"Then, hopefully, they'll take you to Abigail."

"You and I both know that's not the way we want this to play out."

"Yes, but it's a way in."

"She'll want to kill me."

"Maybe, but if Yeshua healed you as you say, do you think he did so only for you to die now?"

Ezekiel thought back to the miraculous story Hadwin had shared by the campfire. Maybe there really was something special about Yeshua. But he couldn't think about that right now. From a glance at Hadwin's face, he could at least tell his words had the desired effect of persuasion.

Familiar surroundings soon came into view. The crosses which littered the outskirts of Tiberias had been removed. While the smell still lingered, it was at least faint.

"It won't be far now." Ezekiel weighed his words. He could see Hadwin struggling. "I meant to say thank you before."

"For what?"

"For agreeing to this crazy plan. For not treating me like the son of a thief . . . or giving up on your family."

"It's nothing you wouldn't do, my boy."

Silence ensued until they came to Ezekiel's house. On the way, Ezekiel had stopped by a stand for some pickled sardines in olive oil. He made a fire in the clay oven and poured some wine. Hadwin drank it so fast Ezekiel thought the man would burst right in front of him.

He knew Abigail frequented the market in Tiberias. The plan was to let certain people know Hadwin was back and where she could find him. He studied his companion's face as they ate. It would be a big gamble. Even though Hadwin was willing to participate, a twinge of guilt grew in Ezekiel's mind.

"Stay here. I'm going into town to let the word out you're here."

The road into town seemed less familiar. Although Ezekiel had walked it thousands of times, the mood of the place seemed different. Coming to the market, he focused on the task at hand. He told a few key people Hadwin's grave had been found empty, that he was reportedly alive, hiding in his abandoned house. The venders he had chosen could be relied upon to spread the news. To make sure they took the bait, he ended each whispered telling of the story with, "Please don't tell anyone."

Ezekiel smiled inwardly as each one vowed to keep the news to themselves. Word would reach Abigail in no time. Before returning home, he bought a new cloak and undergarments for part two of his plan.

"I'm back," he said upon entering the house. But Hadwin didn't turn from his vantage point at the window. He looked out toward the sea.

"How did people receive the news?"

"Everyone was very interested. They won't be able to resist spreading the gossip."

Hadwin seemed to snap out of his reverie. He gathered some reeds to make a decoy. Using the clothes Ezekiel bought, they would make a figure in Hadwin's old house. Time was of the essence. They pulled a wheeled cart along the road toward the abandoned house with their supplies. Ezekiel even brought along a knife to shear hair from Hadwin's head for the dummy. From a distance, it would look like Hadwin was sitting by his clay oven. Both agreed it would be wise to camp out somewhere equidistant from their houses.

Once again, Ezekiel acknowledged to himself the plan's risk factors. The irony of the situation wasn't lost on him either. Here was the man who'd been like a father to him helping him save his real father, who had been absent most of his life. A twinge of guilt resurfaced. What if this didn't go as planned? Was it worth the gamble? Only time would tell. It was too late to turn back now.

The boulder they hid behind provided ample cover while giving them a comfortable place to camp. The day waxed on as the two men sat in as much silence as they could handle. Ezekiel just hoped they wouldn't have to sit there overnight.

Finally, there was movement around the house. They spied a servant boy approaching it with an oil lamp. Within minutes, the house was ablaze.

"I guess we have our answer as to coming in peace," said Hadwin.

But Ezekiel didn't answer. He felt the sharp point of cold steel against his neck.

"Stand up very slowly," said a gruff voice. Ezekiel complied. He saw Hadwin freeze as another man drew a sword to his friend's throat.

"We're going to walk slowly down to the street."

Ezekiel noticed three more armed men nearby. One of them disarmed him, examining his sword.

"You won't do much damage with this!"

The others snickered while Ezekiel rolled his eyes. Hadwin shook visibly. When they came to the street, horses were waiting for the men. There was even one extra.

"Get on the horse. And you, get on behind him," said the leader.

Ezekiel mounted quickly and pulled Hadwin up behind him. One thought comforted him. Abigail wouldn't bring them to her alive, on horseback, if she were just going to kill them. People could see as they rode along, and that would be careless on her part. Abigail didn't strike him as being careless.

The men didn't appear in a hurry either. Ezekiel realized some of them had once worked for Hadwin. He knew they respected him. The horses trotted along at a slow pace until they stopped before Abigail's palatial home. Her mother stood at the entrance, ready to greet them as guests. This was entirely unexpected. Inside, they were ushered to a large reception room where Abigail sat on an ornate chair. The dagger sat in plain view on a stone table before her.

"It was a brave thing you tried to do today. I gained a little bit of respect for you because of it."

"I don't know what to say."

"I was talking to Hadwin," she corrected.

"What do you want?" Hadwin asked.

"What do I want?" She acted as though she'd never pondered that question. Ezekiel knew better. Any man who underestimated Abigail, did so at his own peril.

"I need a manager."

"What makes you think I would ever work for you?"

"Well, I don't believe you have a choice. Out of mercy, I offer to make you my bond slave.

"According to Hebrew tradition or your own?"

"Since I'm half Hebrew, we can use that tradition." She called for a servant.

"But I have to agree to this."

"You know I'm capable of having you put to death if you refuse."

Ezekiel looked at Hadwin in horror.

"What of my family?"

"I have no use for them. They can stay wherever they are. You're never to speak to or see them again."

Tears formed in Hadwin's eyes as he turned to Ezekiel. "I knew the risks."

A servant entered with a small tool in one hand. Ezekiel recognized it as an awl, a tool used for piercing small holes in leather. Two more servants brought Hadwin to the doorpost. Using the awl and a hammer, they pierced his left ear first, then his right.

"Now you belong to me," Abigail said coldly.

As the men took him away, Hadwin yelled to Ezekiel, "Take care of Ester and Rina! Don't let them know where I am!"

Ezekiel felt a heavy hand grasp his arm. After throwing him outside, the servant tossed the dagger at his feet. For a second, he considered attacking the man with it, but it would be suicide. As the door slammed shut, he picked up the dagger, tears forming in his eyes. He hoped this would all be worth it. For now, the only thing he could do was to keep moving. He would go back to Jerusalem.

The way back to Jerusalem was painfully slow. *How am I going to keep this from Rina?* he thought. Clouds filled the sky, though the sky refused to rain. At least the air felt cool to his skin. He already had a late start and no supplies to make camp. Abigail had left his money alone. All he had was his money and the dagger. *At least I can save my father's life.* He walked all through the night. The sun was coming up over the horizon when he finally sat down beside a sycamore tree. Exhausted and guilt-ridden, he let himself go to sleep. He woke when the sun was in the middle of the sky. He checked his cloak. The dagger and his money were still there. Relieved, he rose from his position and trod on. His head felt heavy. His walk was almost a stagger. By the time he saw the city walls of Jerusalem, he felt a burst of energy. Quickening his pace, Ezekiel set out for Elyam's house.

Rina met him at the door.

"Ezekiel! It's so good to see you!"

"You too."

"What's wrong."

"Nothing. I'm just tired."

"Well, I'm sure Elyam has a place for you to rest here."

"Ezekiel, my boy!" said Elyam as he emerged from the back door of the stone house. "You have come back to us. We must celebrate!"

"I'm afraid I'm not up for a celebration tonight," said Ezekiel. "I'm just very tired and need to lie down and rest for a while."

"Sure! Sure! I have a room waiting for you." Elyam led Ezekiel to the back where he could lie down. As his eyelids began to close, he could hear Rina and Elyam talking outside. He positioned himself so he could make out their words.

"Do you think he will ever forgive me?" asked Rina.

Elyam paused for a second. "Rina, Bathshua and I have been married for a long time. Before that we were friends for a long time. All I know is that Ezekiel is a good boy. If he doesn't forgive you yet, he will in time."

"Then why do I feel that I have betrayed him? I did what I thought was right."

"Do you think he bears some guilt as well?"

"What for?"

"Maybe for the shame of who his father is. Rina, you had a wonderful father who loved you and your mother very much. While I tried to be a father to Ezekiel, I could never replace Dismas. It is a wound that doesn't heal easily. Give Ezekiel time. He could have found one of dozens of other girls to be his wife, and yet he has not chosen another. That tells me he still loves you."

"I miss Hadwin." Rina began to cry.

Ezekiel, who wanted sleep desperately, felt his eyes welling up too. He pretended to sleep until sleep finally overtook him.

Ezekiel woke to the smell of bread baking in the clay oven. The smell was heavenly. He was tired of eating pickled fish and drinking cheap wine; oh how he longed for a meal of lamb stew and bread! It was a meal that his mother would make only for special occasions when he was a child. He smiled. Walking into the kitchen area, he stretched his arms up and yawned.

"Well, look who has come in from the long journey," said Ester.

"Smells like it too," said his mother. Her eyes danced, and he knew she was glad to see him.

Ezekiel wanted to ask where Rina was, but he knew it would betray his feelings for her and the regret over asking her father to steal the dagger from Abigail. They would surely be glad to know he was still alive. However, to know they could never see him or speak to him again would be a pain worse than death. *They have already moved on,* he thought. It would be cruel to bring up his being alive right now.

It was not long until Rina arrived with wine purchased at the market. Ezekiel noticed that she smiled, but her eyes did not.

When they sat on the ground for the meal, Elyam regaled them with the story of his donkey waking him up on the trip to Tiberias. He told it with such gusto that even Rina could not help but snap out of her gloom to laugh. *There is the smile that I love,* thought Ezekiel.

After the meal, Ezekiel got up and walked outside. Night had fallen on the city, and the torches were lit for the streets.

"Where are you going?"

Ezekiel turned to face Rina. "Just needed some air."

"Mind if I get some air with you?"

Ezekiel wanted to say that he did mind. He wanted to say a lot of things. But he was respectful. "Do as you wish."

"Do as I wish? Really? We have not seen each other in over a year and a half, and all you can say is 'do as I wish'?"

"What do you want me to say, Rina? Do you want me to say everything is okay?"

"I want you to be honest for once in your life, Ezekiel. You declared your love for me, and now you seem as far away as you ever were."

"A lot has happened."

"A lot has happened to me too, but I am still here."

"I know that. I don't blame you for anything."

"Blame me? Blame . . . me? If anything, I blame you! I would have been happy to be the wife of a poor worker in the fish market if it meant you would be good to me. Whatever happened, we could face it together. But you had to go and sell something that is not yours to build a life I did not want."

"Then why did you agree to marry Asher?"

"Because I wanted you to fight for me!"

"I did! And you know where that got us."

"Yes. I am fully aware of where that got us. The question is, what are we going to do now?"

"I don't know."

"At least you are honest about that."

"You keep talking about honesty, but you know I have never lied to you."

"No, you just lie to yourself, and you want those who love you to lie to you too."

Rina stormed off, leaving Ezekiel there with his guilt exposed. So much for peace and quiet. He decided to walk into town. The atmosphere here was different from Tiberias in that there were more people milling around after dark. Jerusalem had become the trading hub, earning the nickname "the second Rome" from the non-Hebrew travelers.

The streets were lined with vendors, though not as many as during the day. Ezekiel checked to see if his money pouch was still there. The sheath of the dagger dug into his side where it was hidden strapped to his waist underneath his cloak. He knew they took most prisoners to Jerusalem. Since it was the hub of the Jewish world, the Romans knew they would get more attention in the city than they would if they performed their executions in surrounding areas. If an uprising broke out in a particular town, they would execute their prisoners near that town to deter the population from uprising again.

Finding a Roman guard was not difficult. Finding one who was willing to talk to a Hebrew was. Still, he had to try. He found a Roman centurion who was sitting, off duty, on a street corner.

"Hello."

"What do you want?"

"I want to know if there is a prisoner in Jerusalem named Dismas."

"The only way to know is to recognize them at their execution," said the Roman as he took a swig from his wineskin.

"Is there a way to buy them back?"

"No. If they are marked for death, only a pardon from Pontius Pilate can do that."

"Is there a way I can get an audience with him?"

"Not for a Hebrew. If you were a Roman citizen, you could."

"So, I need to find a Roman citizen to go before him."

"If you can. Most Roman citizens would not dare to go before a powerful governor such as him."

"I have to say, you are a lot friendlier than most Romans are to the Hebrews."

"It was a Hebrew who healed my son."

Ezekiel wanted to ask more but didn't want to push his luck.

"Well, you have my thanks. You've been very helpful."

The Roman nodded. Ezekiel left puzzled. *How am I going to get a Roman citizen to advocate for me?* he asked himself.

CHAPTER 34

Hadwin's ears throbbed, but the pain of the piercing was nothing compared to the hopelessness he felt in his soul. The law was not on his side. He had no rights. All he could do was serve a conniving woman who would sooner see him killed than allow him to see his family. He spent the nights in chains and the mornings in plain sight of her most trusted guards. Escape was out of the question.

Each night he prayed that God would avenge him and set him free to be with his family. He remembered the teachings of the synagogue on Joseph. Hadwin hoped this was a test from God, but he feared it was just an unfortunate circumstance.

When the command came through the guards that Abigail wanted an audience with her new slave, it took the ranks by surprise. Most of the servants and slaves were there only to serve Abigail and her mother. They did not receive an audience.

The ornate furnishings of the hall reminded Hadwin of the Temple in Jerusalem. He walked with the men to a place where Abigail was reclining.

"Leave us," she told the servants.

Hadwin could see a tear forming in the corner of her eye.

"I hope you understand, I had to save face with the servants. One moment of weakness, and they will turn on me."

"Spoken like a true Roman," said Hadwin.

"Only half. My mother had a lover who was a Samaritan. Asher was my half-brother."

"Well, what do you want with a Hebrew? Now that I am a bondslave, you own me."

"I will set you free if you can gain me an audience with Yeshua. I met him once, and I must get to know him."

"That is what this is about? Last I heard he was headed to Jerusalem."

"You must know him. He doesn't get called out in the middle of the night to heal someone he doesn't know."

"The truth of the matter is . . ." Hadwin thought for a second. "I do know him, but I haven't seen him in some time."

"Then tell me, how do I get an audience with him?"

"Set me free for three days. I can get close to him. Then I will bring him back to you."

"Do you believe me to be simple? Am I stupid? You would be gone in a moment, and I would have to expend enormous energy hunting you down. I will accompany you to Judea. Then you will have no choice but to follow the commands I give. The servants will shear your hair, so there will be no question about the fact you are a bondslave."

"You enjoy torturing people, don't you?"

"That's enough!" said Abigail. "You will do as I say. If you want to live."

"What if I said I don't?"

"Guards!" Two men came into the room. Abigail waited for a moment. Then, as if a fire ignited, she brightened up. "Kill him!"

The men drew their swords.

"Wait! I didn't say I want to die . . . I said what if."

"Hold it." Abigail motioned for the men to stop. "I know this is your first day, so I will be kind. You do not have a say. You will speak when spoken to. You will not lash out in any way if you want to live long enough to see your wretched family again."

"I understand."

Abigail motioned to her guard. He took the pummel of his sword and slammed it into Hadwin's back, sending him sprawling to the floor.

"Speak when you are spoken to!" she said. "Take him back to his quarters. Make sure he can travel tomorrow."

The men threw him into his makeshift dungeon and put him back in his chains. Hadwin remained motionless until the men left. Then, under the cover of darkness, he smiled. There was a hidden promise that he would see his family again.

CHAPTER 35

Abigail went to her quarters as well. She felt something else. A twinge of pity. Hadwin was different from the other men she encountered in her life. He would die for his family. Another emotion crept into her mind. Jealousy. She shouldn't be jealous of this man. The only person she would die for was her mother, who would likely die in the next few years anyway. Even so, the anger that accompanied these emotions still stirred, causing her to feel unsure of her calculated ways.

Abigail decided she needed to see this rabbi who had told of her past. She didn't know why she was drawn to him. Everything in her life up to this point was about survival. She raged against being a tool for fortune making. Now it was her fortune, and she felt even worse. Suicide was an option. She contemplated it often. She planned on using the dagger she bought in the market, but now Ezekiel had it.

She knew these were fantasies. Just a way to dream about ending her own pain and suffering. The truth was, she was too afraid to do something like that. She saw the fear in her brother's eyes as she choked the life out of him. She saw the sadness when she murdered her servant who lied about Hadwin. No matter how she justified those killings, they haunted her. She barely slept. Maybe that was what she needed now. They would travel to Jerusalem in the morning. She heard the famous rabbi was going there next.

She drank some of the stronger wine from her vineyard until she fell asleep.

The next morning came with a vengeance. Abigail crawled from her bed to get ready for the journey. She would take only three servants with her—two guards and Hadwin. Her head was exploding, and light seemed to make it worse. Taking her head covering, she wrapped her head in such a way that she could only look through a narrow slit to reduce the glare of the sunlight. Her servants had already sheared Hadwin's head. He was in shackles. She mounted her horse, and the servants pulled her horse caravan style. Hadwin bounced along on a donkey behind her.

The going was slow and steady. Abigail noticed the absence of crosses. With Passover coming in a couple of weeks, the Roman overlords must have wanted to be respectful of the local traditions. She knew that, however cruel the Romans were, they were also pragmatic. There was no use in inciting needless violence and protests. Each people group they subjugated was allowed to practice their own religion and elect their own local leaders, as long as they recognized the sovereignty of Rome.

The people they passed seemed happy to go about their business. Abigail wondered why everyone seemed happy just to exist. Her entire life existence had seemed like giving up. She had been abused, married into loveless marriages, and encouraged just to go along. When she finally found the courage to take action, she vowed never to be a slave again. She also vowed never to feel or care for others again. She had stuffed everything down so far that when she started to feel again it made her dangerous. Now she ended lives, making her godlike, but she felt worse than ever before. She would never let on that she could feel again.

CHAPTER 36

Elyam went to the Jerusalem market to get supplies for the upcoming Passover. He went two weeks early to try to beat the crowds this time of year. Even so it would be nearly impossible to get everything he needed. He walked along the crowded street up to the Temple Mount. After buying his provisions and loading his donkey, he walked in the direction of his home. The bags of grain and jugs of wine were almost too much for the donkey, which brayed under the load. With patience, Elyam led the donkey slowly through the street. The donkey's progress was so slow that Elyam decided he had to find a place to sit and rest for a moment. He surveyed the crowd as he pulled out an old wineskin. Taking a few swigs and looking around, he overheard someone's conversation.

"Did you hear? That rabbi who claims he is the Messiah is coming to Jerusalem next week. They say he will overthrow the Romans."

"I did hear that. He had better be careful. The Romans don't like talk like that."

"We're planning a rally when he rides into the city. Invite all of those who are sympathetic to the cause."

"Excuse me, sir, did you say he's coming here next week?" said Elyam.

"Why, yes. I guess I better be more careful about how loud I say these things."

"It's alright. I would like my family to be involved if we can."

"Well, just show up and bring something you can wave in the air. If enough people show up, then maybe Pilate will have to listen to us."

"One can only pray," said Elyam. When he felt like he had rested enough he led his donkey through the crowd. Upon arriving home, he unloaded his supplies and kissed Bathshua on the cheek.

"I believe this is going to be the most memorable Passover celebration yet."

"What makes you say that?"

"Oh, just something I heard in the city."

Elyam sat on a wooden bench. He needed rest, and it was still early in the day. Bathshua brought him a bowl of dried dates.

"Thank you, my dear."

"Well, I know that this year is going to be bigger. Ezekiel might be coming. And, well, it seems that many of our friends will be stopping by."

"That's not what I'm talking about. I hear that Yeshua is going to be here, and he is staying through Passover."

"Here, or in Jerusalem?"

"Jerusalem. Not here. I don't know what we would do if he came here."

"According to the rumors, you could just give him some fish and a little bread, and five thousand people would be fed."

"This is no time for jokes. I know that the Sanhedrin are not happy about it. It seems his popularity with the common folks is a threat to their power."

"They see everything as a threat to their power." Elyam took a swig from his wineskin. Bathshua continued grinding grain on the stone and making bread. He rose from his perch and walked up behind her. Hugging her gently, he whispered into her ear, "I don't know what's going to happen, but I know it's going to be really big. In my prayers I felt God speaking to me."

"I believe you. I know it will be tough for a while, but we always get through." Bathshua smiled and put her hand on his. The flour left a mark, so she touched his face. Laughing, Elyam dipped his hands in the flour and chased her outdoors where they saw Rina, Ester, and Aaliyah walking up the path. Straightening up, Elyam hid his hands behind his back.

"Hi, ladies," he said. Bathshua could not hide her laughter. The three women looked at each other and then back at the grandparents.

With one quick motion Elyam took his flour-laden hands and rubbed them on Aaliyah's face as well, causing Aaliyah and Rina to run into the house and grab fistfuls of flour and chase each other.

"Come on, we are all adults here. We should not act like children," said Ester. At that moment a fistful of flour exploded onto her tunic. A smile spread across her face as she chased her daughter all around the outside of the house.

Each one laughed so hard it seemed their sides would split open. It was as if a great weight lifted off their souls.

Looking up Rina saw Ezekiel coming up the road. "Ezekiel!" She ran to him. Giving her a hug, he greeted the rest of the family.

"What's going on here?" said Ezekiel.

"Oh, we were just having a bit of fun," said Elyam. He could see that Ezekiel was forcing a smile. "Alright, everyone, let's get cleaned up and tonight we will celebrate Ezekiel finally coming home to Jerusalem."

Each of the women went inside to clean up, leaving Elyam and Ezekiel outside to talk.

"I can see you've not lost your enthusiasm for life," said Ezekiel.

"Ezekiel, it is why I have lived so long. You need to learn to lighten up a little. Yahweh did not make us for pain, he made us to enjoy life."

"I wish I had your spirit, Grandpa."

"You are a lot like your mother. You work very hard, and sometimes I see the joy of your work in your eyes. As for me, I am too old to work so hard," said the old man. Ezekiel smiled. His grandfather could always put him at ease in any situation. When the women were finished, the men went in to clean up.

At the evening meal they laughed at Elyam's story of his trip back to Tiberias. The mood was lighter than Ezekiel remembered. The secret of Hadwin's captivity etched its way into his mind, and he forced himself to be happy. They all stayed up late talking about old times and people they once knew.

The next day Ezekiel woke with a start. He had missed his family so much. He didn't realize how much until his return. He was thankful for one night of peace.

Still, when everyone was asleep, he could sense himself boiling. Each thought was of Hadwin. He had to make good on his promise. He had to save his father, protect Rina and Ester. The weight was now on him. He had no idea how he would accomplish this. If the idea of marching up to a Roman guard and trying to facilitate the exchange of the dagger for his father seemed crazy, it's because it was. The Romans were an elite force, and even their prison guards were tougher than most. He would need to be patient, find the right moment, and buy his father out of prison. It was not unheard of. Many of the social elites had bought their way out of prison. Ezekiel hoped the dagger would be enough.

Sleep eluded him for most of the night. Only when the first rays of the rising sun poked their way through the window opening did he finally fall asleep. The rest of the family rose with the sun. They knew Ezekiel was exhausted, and so they each did their best not to wake him.

CHAPTER 37

Hadwin rode his horse in a slow and steady plod behind Abigail. He had not said much to her since his captivity, only enough to stay out of trouble. He knew there was an ulterior motive behind her "kindness," and with each clop of a hoof he knew he should escape. The problem was that now he would look like an escaped slave, a crime that brought severe punishments. The physical signs of his slavery—the shaved head and pierced ears—would be a dead giveaway that he was on the run. Still, he thanked God that he was alive. Hope, however slight, trickled into his soul. He was going to Jerusalem. He might see his family again.

"Keep up!" shouted Abigail. Hadwin quickened the pace of his horse.

"I'm doing my best here."

"Shut up! You are now a slave. You only speak to me when I ask you to."

Everything in Hadwin wanted to fight back. He knew it would not end well here.

"You know I could serve you better as an adviser rather than a slave."

Abigail motioned to one of her guards. He rode his horse back to where Hadwin had stopped. Pulling out a whip, he lashed it across Hadwin's back. The wooden hooks woven into the leather straps dug into his flesh, pulling him to the ground. A hot streak of pain shot through Hadwin's whole body as he lay on the ground. He looked up. Abigail was enjoying this. She sat on her horse staring at the spectacle.

"Get up," he heard her say in the distance. The throbbing in his head reminded him of the Roman war drums he heard as a child when the Roman legions embarked on a new war. He tried to get up, but his body revolted. He felt two sets of hands pull him to his feet.

"I'm not going to tell you again. You address me when I ask you to."

He tried to get back on his horse, but he was too weak. One of the guards grabbed him around his legs and hoisted him to the back of the animal. Slowly Hadwin was able to get his legs situated on the animal and sit up.

"We've lost enough time here. Let's keep moving," said Abigail. Once they neared the city of Jerusalem, Hadwin could see the familiar site of the Temple Mount overlooking the narrow streets and marketplaces. His ears still throbbed. He could barely keep his eyes open even while riding on the back of the animal. His plan was to cut his earlobes off once he found a time when he could escape. Then he could blame it on the cruelty of robbers who thought they could have a laugh at his expense. He knew it was not likely to be successful, but he had to try. Hadwin had no intention of being a captive for very long. He could not figure out why Abigail was in such a hurry. Yeshua would likely be in Jerusalem through Passover.

The crowds of people began to gather in numbers Hadwin had never seen before. He could see that it made Abigail nervous. The crowds were so large that Abigail and the guards dismounted to lead the horses through. Hadwin didn't want to walk. He had not recovered from the beating. However, his better judgment took control and he dismounted, groaning the whole time. Everyone had palm leaves in their hands. *How peculiar*, he thought. Then the crowds parted, and people were throwing their coats on the ground. He could barely see a man on a donkey. The crowd cheered so loud that it hurt Hadwin's ears. He recognized Yeshua. It made him smile. The people were shouting phrases like "Here comes the Messiah to save God's people from tyranny!"

Hadwin knew language like that could get someone killed. The Romans did not like anyone challenging their power. It did not matter whether he claimed to be divine or not. Following through the crowd, Abigail and her guards kept moving. Hadwin thought if he could make a run for it then he could possibly be free. However, he didn't know how Abigail would make his family suffer if he did. He pushed himself through the crowd to catch up to the guards. It was better that he make his escape when they were not in Jerusalem. They stayed until the crowd died down.

Hadwin tried to find an inn that was not fully occupied. Each house he went to had no vacancies. It was the week before Passover, and people loved to travel to Jerusalem during this time. Finally he found one inn with a stable that had a vacancy. Only enough for the guards and Abigail. Hadwin had to stay with the animals. He didn't mind too much. It took the pressure off having to bend to their every whim.

Even in the lights of the city the stable was dark, allowing him to sleep. The bed of straw he made was a welcome reprieve from the ground on which he normally slept. The smell from the animals, on the other hand, was bad enough to wake the dead. Even so, the dead of night and total exhaustion took over, and his eyes closed and did not open until light made its appearance from behind the leather window coverings.

His whole body ached as he picked himself up. His back was still tender from the lashing, and he knew he would get another one if he failed to have their provisions ready to move out.

"Why didn't you run?"

Hadwin turned around to see Abigail standing in the entryway. "I don't know what you mean," he said.

"You could have run. There are ways of hiding your earlobes. Why didn't you?"

Hadwin paused for a moment, weighing his words carefully. "You know what my family looks like. I have no doubt you will find them if I anger you. So I stayed."

His words hung in the air.

"You truly love your daughter," said Abigail. It was almost a question.

"She is my whole world. I would die for her."

"And Ester, your wife?"

"Her as well."

Hadwin went back to his work. He could feel her eyes staring at him, looking for something. A tell. A moment of weakness.

"You know I never had a father. I should say I never had a father who cared at all for his daughter."

Hadwin stayed silent. He kept packing the horses with the provisions they had left.

Abigail turned to walk away. Hadwin saw an opportunity.

"Wait! Tell me. What would you have done if I had run?"

"I would have added you to a long list of men who have abandoned me. Then I would've hunted you down and had you killed."

"You cannot buy a father's love. You know that."

"Who says I wanted to?"

"You did when you could have had me killed. Instead, you wanted to come to Jerusalem to see Yeshua. Why?"

"I don't know."

"I think you do know. I think you want what Ester and Rina have, but you don't have the tools to find it yourself."

"I don't want you to be my father, if that is what you're saying."

"No, you just want to believe that some men can be kind. You want to know that someone out there actually cares what happens to you."

"So, do you? Do you care?"

Hadwin paused for a moment. "I am a bondslave, am I not?"

Abigail smiled for a moment. And for a moment, Hadwin thought he spied a flicker of humanity in her eyes. "Well, there are men who can be kind, but I am incapable of kindness."

Hadwin waited for the next sentence, which inevitably would be his sentence. It never came. He saw a tear roll down Abigail's cheek. He was confused by his own emotions. Why and how could he feel compassion for such a creature? This woman was why his family was in hiding. She was the reason he gave up his old life to spare their lives. This woman killed some of his friends. Yet, for a moment, he felt compassion for her. Even worse, he saw Rina in her eyes.

Everything he had said was to survive. Yet there was a twinge of authenticity in his voice. A longing for normalcy that he could not hide. When he looked at Abigail, all he saw was a hurt child—a woman who had been abused by life and a survivor. He had to escape.

CHAPTER 38

E zekiel grew adept at faking a smile. He knew Rina could read him; he was not fooling her. Still, he gave it his best effort. His mother was glad to have him around, and he could tell she felt more at ease, even with Ester and Rina. He brought some money, which was added to the coffers in the house that helped to provide for everyone. It was a small fraction of the money he kept on him. He was also careful to hide the dagger. It puzzled him that this half-breed woman would keep her promise to him. She had no reason to give the dagger to him. She could have easily made a bondservant out of him as well.

The preparations for Passover were one of the times he enjoyed most during the year. Everyone was happy that week, celebrating God passing over the houses of the faithful to vanquish the enemies of the people of God. This time of year gave him hope that God, if he was real, could do the same with the Romans. Yet he could not bring himself to thank a God who had let his father be led away in chains and injustice be done to God's chosen people. While he no longer believed in a pantheon of gods, he decided that God must be cruel if he existed.

It took him three times longer for each task than usual. The crushing weight of finding his father and caring for those he loved left him feeling empty. The most crushing element? Leaving Hadwin to his fate with Abigail. He would have to mount a rescue once the dust settled. He didn't know if it was arrogance or desperation that assured him that he was capable of such a task. Ezekiel was also afraid that his family would find him out. Pushing himself, he threw himself into chores so he could keep his mind off things.

He noticed Rina eying him suspiciously. He kept working, fixing the doorpost that was rotting away. He would be on the roof next, for a leak had formed in the rain. He turned his eyes from her gaze.

"You can't avoid me this whole time. We are going to have to talk eventually," said Rina.

"Nothing to talk about," said Ezekiel.

"So that is how you are, just shutting me out? Nothing to talk about?"

"No. Nothing at all."

"Did you ever think there might be some things I need to say?"

"I think you said all you needed to say the other day."

"You surprised me. I don't like surprises. You should know that."

"You see, there you go. All of a sudden, I am the bad guy. You agreed to marry Asher. If it weren't for your father, you would be married to him right now."

Rina tried to gain her composure before answering. She failed.

"Yes, and not a day goes by that I don't think about that. I am the one who got him killed. I have to live with that! But you have to remember who you are. You are the son of a thief who was not willing to take on the stigma. But at some point, you also have to realize that you are not your father."

Ezekiel looked at her. His eyes betrayed his smirk as his face twisted in agony. "You know nothing of who I am."

"Oh really! I know nothing. We grew up together, Ezekiel. You have very few other friends who can say the same. Our families are closer than relatives. And you say I know nothing of who you are. You know, I think you have lost who you are."

She was right, and Ezekiel was very aware of the truth. A part of him died when he saw Rina in Asher's arms. His whole life had been her. Everything he did was for her. Now her words pierced him like a dagger. He laid down his mallet and walked away. She called for him, and he ignored her. Anger boiled in his soul. *How dare she talk to me like that?* he thought. The path was familiar. It was like every road leading away from Jerusalem. He blamed Rina for all the pain he now felt. Not because she was guilty, but because his pain needed a target and she was the easiest one. Anything to keep from blaming himself. Tears flowed down his cheeks, a sensation he had not felt in quite a while.

Up ahead he noticed a crowd. They were shouting "Hosanna!" and waving branches. A lone figure on a donkey rode ahead.

He recognized him and hid. "I don't want to see him right now," he said under his breath. Then it hit him. Yeshua prophesied that someone was going to die. Was it Hadwin? His stomach sank. He did not need another death on his head. God, or the gods, would never forgive him. He found a back alley in an effort to get away. The crowd moved right by the alley. But when he looked up, he found Yeshua had stopped and looked at him for a moment. Ezekiel froze. The sadness in Yeshua's eyes was unmistakable. Then Yeshua clicked his heels and the crowd followed him through town. It was a few moments before Ezekiel allowed himself to move again.

Why was Yeshua sad? Everyone was praising him. Everyone looked happy to see him. Was this the revolution? Was this the moment when the Romans would be overthrown? No, it couldn't be. The Romans were too powerful. Many nations tried and failed to overthrow the most powerful government in the world. Still, there was a growing movement. *How foolish are they?* he thought. He walked out of town another way. He wanted to run away, never to return.

A man walking in the opposite direction of the crowd stopped for a moment.

"Ezekiel?" It was Sittish.

"Hello, Sittish," said Ezekiel. Not wanting to belabor the conversation, Ezekiel searched his mind for an excuse to get away.

"How are you my friend? You look good."

"I'm doing alright," said Ezekiel.

"You don't sound alright," Sittish said.

"I am fine . . . really."

"Well, let's see if there is a place to get something to eat around here," said Sittish. "I know a stand that sells bread and figs."

Ezekiel sighed and nodded. He followed the Hittite through the crowd to a place where they could each buy something to eat.

"So where are your men?"

"They returned home. Yeshua's teachings were a little too radical for them."

"So, what is he teaching now?" asked Ezekiel as they found a place along the road to sit and talk.

"Many of them don't like the idea of forgiving your enemies. We have many enemies, and they have perpetrated unspeakable crimes against our people. So, they left." Sittish smiled and popped a date into his mouth.

"So why are you still here?" Ezekiel asked.

"I'm not sure I know how to answer that question. His way of teaching intrigues me. I think it is a nice thought, forgiving others," said Sittish.

"Someone with your skill with a sword doesn't have to."

"You know, you are the lucky one. You have not killed anyone. You don't have to live with the fact that you have taken someone's life," said Sittish.

"Believe me. I have a lot I have to live with." Ezekiel sighed.

Sittish paused for a moment. "I guess that is why I am here. It is my last hope for forgiveness. If God or the gods look down on murder, and I think they do, then I am alright. If they look down on killing, then I am not." A tired look came over his face. Ezekiel knew this look. He saw it in Hadwin's face when he was conscripted into being a bondslave. He saw this moments before in the face of Yeshua. Now he saw it in Sittish as he told of having to kill and hating himself for it.

Ezekiel listened, but his thoughts drifted off as if some cloud covered the recesses of his mind. He failed to notice the sword at Sittish's side. It was a Roman Gladius. Superb in balance and the main weapon of the centurion guard, if he had noticed it, he would have seen what was coming next. Instead, he said his goodbye and set off for home. Looking down the street he saw a group of Roman guards in formation running toward Sittish—standing like a lone warrior with the Gladius in one hand and his Hittite inspired sword in the other.

Ezekiel could only watch as the Romans threw a javelin, which Sittish cut down easily, distracting him from the blow of a centurion sneaking up from behind. The man was easily overcome by the highly trained Romans and forced to the ground and put into chains. Immediately Ezekiel knew why the man had no followers left. They were a band of thieves, and either they were caught or killed. The Romans would take this thief and make an example of him.

Ezekiel turned away and kept walking. He did not want to be associated with this thief.

CHAPTER 39

Elyam wanted to see if the repairs to the house were done. When he came to the side of their home, he found Rina still working.

"Where is Ezekiel?"

"I don't know," said Rina.

"What do you mean?"

"He left. We talked. He got mad and left," she said.

"I see."

Elyam stayed quiet for the next few moments.

"I don't get it. Every time I want to have a conversation with him, he just walks away."

Elyam looked up from his work, sighed, and then walked over to Rina.

"For the few years your father was on this earth, you knew he was a good man. You knew he loved you more than anything. Right?"

"Yes?"

"Ezekiel never knew that from his father. His whole life he has been fighting, trying to overcome the stigma of being the son of a thief. I'm afraid it's a wound that does not heal fully."

"I know he is different from his father."

"Yes, but he doesn't know that. He lives with fear that he will never measure up to your expectations, or anyone else's for that matter. The good news is he hasn't given up on trying. Have you told him that you love him?"

"That would not be proper!" said Rina.

"Well, Ezekiel has never been one to care about proper. I am just saying that it might be what it takes to reach him." Elyam went back to working on the doorpost that Ezekiel left. He could see a tear escape the corner of Rina's eye.

"I wish you kids would just realize that you love each other. You are made for each other."

"You think so?"

"I do, child. Love is never easy. But it is worth it." Elyam finished his work and walked away. When he turned the corner, he met Bathshua staring at him.

"What?" Elyam said.

"You were made for each other? Are you trying to meddle in our grandson's affairs?" she said with a smile.

"I would like to know my grandchildren someday. Sometimes these kids need a little push. You know?" he smiled back.

"Well, be careful. Let Yahweh take care of them. He will bring them together."

"I hope you are right."

"Of course, I am right, my dear. Every story has its dark days before the light. Why don't you help me bake the bread," said Bathshua.

Elyam did as he was told. The day seem to melt into the night.

Ezekiel took his time coming home. He hoped that everyone would be asleep by the time he got there. He was wrong. Elyam was waiting for him. The oil lamp he was holding cast shadows on every wrinkle of his face.

"I suppose you are going to lecture me now."

"Wouldn't dream of it. Did I ever tell you of my journey to Egypt?"

Ezekiel was surprised. He thought he had heard every one of his grandfather's stories.

"No, I don't believe so."

"Well, it is one I don't tell very often. It is when I met Bathshua. By the way, Bathshua is her Hebrew name. Her Egyptian name was Nefertiti. It means beauty has arrived. Her father was wanting to sell her because he incurred some debts. Oh, was she beautiful! She was bid on by everyone of substance. Some of these men had five or six wives already. So, when it came time for me to bid, I decided to do something different. I didn't want to buy a wife. I wanted to be chosen by a wife. So, I made the highest bid. She nearly cost me everything I owned. Her father gave her to me, and I told him I wanted to have a Hebrew wedding, which could only be performed by a Rabbi. He agreed, and since there were no Rabbis in Egypt, he said that she should travel with me to Jerusalem.

"That night I came to Nefertiti and told her that she was free to leave and do as she wished. That I would never pay for a wife, I was merely paying for her freedom. She agreed to travel with me to Jerusalem and would make her decision there. She later told me that I made her feel wanted in a way she had never felt before. Every other person who bid on her made her feel like she was property. She never felt she was of any value. When she found out how much her freedom had cost me, she told me she would spend a lifetime to pay me back. I would not let her do that. So for the next few months she lived in my guest house. She allowed other men to court her, and boy was I jealous. But I knew that if she were to choose me, I would have a love that would last a lifetime. Finally, she came to me and said, 'I am ready.' 'For what?' I asked. She said, 'To make your people my people.' I knew then that she had chosen, not just me, but to make a life with me. She was baptized before Yahweh and her name was changed to Bathshua. She became my wife, and I have lived the happiest life with her that I could ever hope for."

"So, you are saying I shouldn't get angry because Rina chose another."

"She was forced into slavery. Circumstances brought her out of it. I am sorry for Hadwin. I think she still grieves for him."

All the blood drained from Ezekiel's face. He had taken away the one chance for Rina to have her father back.

"I don't think Rina would choose me."

"Only if you would not choose yourself. Ask yourself, if you were Rina, would you choose you? I think you probably would. You are a hard worker. Provider. I believe she loves you."

"If you knew half the things I've done, you wouldn't think so."

"Ezekiel, no one in this world is innocent. Some are just better than others at hiding it. Rina loves you. The question is do you love her enough to give her the choice?" Elyam rose from his seated position with a groan. "I am tired. I think I'll go to bed now."

———

The next morning, Ezekiel rose with a start. He had overslept. The sun was now in full color, and the family was milling about doing chores. Wiping his eyes and shaking his head, he felt as though he had too much wine the night before. He decided to return to the work he was doing the day before, but to his surprise it was already done. *Elyam needed me and I let him down*, he thought.

He walked outside where he saw Elyam stacking firewood for the oven.

"Will you let me do the heavy work?"

"Since when am I so feeble that I can't do heavy work. Do you think I'm old?"

"Well, you're not in your youth anymore, and I can help take care of this kind of stuff."

"I like this kind of work. I think you should talk to Rina. She's cleaning right now and could use a break. And don't run away this time. She might say something you need to hear," said Elyam.

Ezekiel scowled and left. He found Rina in the house cleaning, just as Elyam said. It was funny that he hadn't noticed her when he walked outside.

"Are you going to say something or just stand there like a dullard," said Rina.

"I'm sorry. For, ah, yesterday. I was not feeling well and . . ." He couldn't get the words out. He was so disgusted by his own behavior that he didn't have the words to say.

"I never told you that I'm . . . glad you came back. It's nice to have you around again," said Rina.

"It's good to see you too. I see a husband has not snatched you up yet."

"Only because I'm holding on to hope that a certain man would take me as his wife."

"Does this man know that you want him in your life?"

"I don't know. I think he might be a little slow," said Rina. Her stern face gave the slightest hint of a wry smile.

"A lot has happened since we were kids."

"I know," Rina said softly.

"Do you think we could ever just go back?"

"To what?"

"To where we were just happy to be near each other." Ezekiel searched her eyes for a moment. Why didn't she say anything?

"No," said Rina.

Ezekiel's heart sank. His mind furiously tried to come up with an explanation for why she said they couldn't go back. Did she love him? Did she forget all the good times they had? Was she past the point where they could have a future?

"I love being around you, Ezekiel, but if you're chasing a feeling, then we will never work. I don't want someone I have to fix. I want someone who knows who he is and is willing to do what it takes to win me. I don't want to be someone's property."

Inside Ezekiel wanted to cry. Outwardly he forced a smile and tried not to show his disappointment.

"You would never be my property. You know I could love you very much."

"You don't even love yourself. How could you ever love me that much?"

Ezekiel didn't have an answer for Rina. He knew she was right. Only he knew how wounded he felt at every moment. It was as if someone had poured hot pitch all over him, and the slightest touch hurt. He was closed off from others. He lived inside his head and never allowed his heart to reveal itself. He wanted nothing and everything from his father, who was never there. He wanted to see him one more time, to tell him how he felt and that he had learned to become a man from others and not from him. That he was both proud and ashamed to be his son.

Now he was standing in front of the only woman he ever loved, unsure if he could love her in the way that she deserved.

"I'm sorry, Zeke. I don't know what came over me," said Rina.

Ezekiel couldn't help but show the hurt in his face. And he couldn't walk away. If he did then Elyam would have been right. He would just run when things turned out wrong. Like his father did. He did not want to be like his father. So, he stood there. He didn't say anything. He just stood, looking at Rina in disbelief.

Ezekiel sat down in the middle of the room. He weighed what he would say in his head, but nothing sounded right. All he could do was sit there and wait for the next verbal arrow to pierce his ego again. It didn't come. Rina stared back at him with those beautiful brown eyes. She had just told him she wanted him to take her as his wife, and in the same interaction she said he couldn't love her.

"Please don't run away again. We all need you, Ezekiel. I need you. I just need you to be the man you could be," she said in a softer tone. She almost said the words he wanted to hear. Those three words that would have made all the difference. But she didn't. And he couldn't bring himself to utter them as well. The silence of the moment was deafening. Rina slowly walked out of the room. Ezekiel smiled. His heart jumped in his chest, a feeling he hadn't felt since he first held her hand—when he knew he wanted her forever and would do whatever it took to make her his.

CHAPTER 40

Two days later, the preparations for Passover were ramping up. Ezekiel once loved this time of year; however, this time he had a feeling. An awful feeling. Like when a parent knows their child is guilty of something and the truth has not come out in the open. Something was wrong. Try as he might, he couldn't hide behind his fake smile and be charming like his grandfather. *How does he do it?* he thought. *He has the whole world listening to one of his crazy stories, and their troubles melt away.* Ezekiel wanted to be like that, but he just couldn't. His face couldn't hide the trouble in his heart.

Still early in the morning, the sunlight was peaking its way through the buildings. Somehow the air felt fresher in the morning. In the city people moved quickly to set up their stands and bring their goods to market. Ezekiel felt a little better. Each breath felt like new life in his lungs, and he was able to push his troubles to the recesses of his mind. The way to Herod's Temple was relatively quiet as this was a somber week for the Jews—a reminder that the death angel had "passed over" every Hebrew house marked with the blood of a lamb, and a celebration that Yahweh had led them out of slavery and into the Promised Land.

He had grown accustomed to doing his own thing, working hard and having all the time in the world to himself. Now, with so many people in the household, he felt smothered. He walked along alone with his thoughts for quite some time. He didn't know what to do now that he didn't have to be out early in the morning to fish. Work was his outlet. With that out of the way, he felt lost. The work of the household seemed meaningless.

He thought it might not hurt to buy the animal that would be sacrificed for the sins of the family that week, so he went to the front gate of the Temple. There he saw Yeshua taking vines and braiding them. He was visibly angry.

"I wouldn't go in there if I were you."

"Why not?"

Yeshua just looked straight ahead and walked through the gates shouting and turning over the tables. His disciples who had already entered the Temple tried to calm him down.

"It was written that this is supposed to be a house of prayer! Now you have turned it into a den of thieves!" Yeshua shouted. The merchants who were buying and selling began to pick up their coins and merchandise. Some left them there on the Temple floor, too scared to stay. Doves flew from the tables in a circle. Their clipped wings kept them at eye level and they seemed to find the face of everyone who was trying to catch the lambs that were released. Other venders tried to stand in the gate but the sheer number of animals that were released overwhelmed them. Curse words flew as the men tried to redeem the flocks. Ezekiel just stood there amused at the spectacle.

Yeshua pushed past him, saying, "See, I told you that you don't want to go in there." Ezekiel was so surprised that a chuckle came from under his breath. Most of the Jews resented the moneychangers for charging their high prices and taking advantage of the lower classes. Ezekiel decided to go to the outskirts of Jerusalem to buy his animals. It would be the first time in a long time that Elyam, as the head of the family, presented the lambs. Most of the time they had to present doves for they were less expensive.

It was not long before Ezekiel found a farmer who was selling lambs suitable for the Day of Atonement. He paid his four coins and walked back to their house with the new animal.

CHAPTER 41

It was difficult for Hadwin to be so close to his family and yet not allowed to see them. He worked hard, knowing that his only hope was to find himself in Abigail's good graces. He knew she relished her control over him, and as long as he did as she wished he would survive long enough for Yeshua to free him. They stayed at the inn, which was just as well. He could clean the stable enough to feel comfortable to sleep, and whatever Abigail was searching for, he hoped she found it soon. Her guards put him in shackles each night. Each morning they released them and went back to sleep as he fed the horses and did their work for them.

He had learned in this world that if he did more than expected, he would have an easier life. This particular morning, as he was performing his chores, Abigail came to see him.

"Saddle up my horse. I'm going into the city. I will need you to lead me through, so saddle up two horses."

"Shall I wake your guards?"

"I don't think so. If you haven't run yet, then I believe you will stay."

"Why are you doing this? You have everything you could possibly want in Tiberias."

"I don't have to answer your questions, slave," said Abigail.

Hadwin, unfazed, stated, "If you were going to kill me you would have already done so. Now we are going into Jerusalem looking for a faith healer. What do you need healing from?"

Abigail stayed silent this time and walked out of the stable to the fresh air outside. Hadwin did as he was told and emerged from the stable with two horses saddled with Roman saddles. Adjusting his cloak as a hood, he led Abigail to the main streets of Jerusalem. The pieces of wood inserted into his earlobes rubbed his neck raw as his horse plodded down the path. The streets were crowded with people who were all looking forward to the final Passover meal and celebration of their release from slavery to the Egyptians.

Hadwin could see the Temple Mount ahead and knew if Yeshua were still in Jerusalem, he would most likely be somewhere near it. As they neared the Temple, they passed lambs and oxen just roaming the streets. Yeshua and his followers were walking through the streets behind them as if he were driving them away from the Temple. The people around him seemed as if they had witnessed a traumatizing event. Hadwin called out, "Yeshua, my mistress needs your assistance. Will you please talk to her?"

Yeshua walked over to where they were mounted. Abigail dismounted her horse. Hadwin held her reins as she approached Yeshua.

Yeshua looked at her and back at Hadwin. "Life has taken a few turns since I last saw you, Hadwin."

"Yes, well, we all do what we need to do to survive. Right?"

Yeshua nodded. "Abigail? Why are you seeking me out?"

Abigail paused for a moment. "I really don't know."

"I think you do. I believe you are looking for a kind of healing you cannot get anywhere else."

Abigail just looked at him. Tears formed as she knelt to the ground. Hadwin could see she was trembling.

"I felt something when talking to you that I have never felt before."

"You have felt it before. It has just been a very long time. You see, Abigail, when you push guilt aside over time you begin to think your behavior is normal."

Yeshua signaled his followers to walk away for the moment.

"I don't know what to say."

"That is the first true statement I've heard coming from you."

"What should I do to become good again?"

"You can't, Abigail. No one is good enough. But there is a way, and will be coming soon, that you can be good again. Why do you want Hadwin as a bondservant?"

"I don't think I can answer that."

"When you want to be honest with yourself, then you can be honest with me. That is when we need to talk."

Yeshua turned to walk away.

"Why don't you command her to release me?" asked Hadwin.

Yeshua turned to face Hadwin. "When you are ready to leave, you will be released. Remember, there is a purpose. It's bigger than your reality now." Hadwin scowled. He didn't want to be in this position. Still afraid Abigail would hurt his family, Hadwin decided to ride the situation out.

"So, you want to be released?" said Abigail. "Then know if you are released, I will hunt you down and when you least expect it, your family will fall into an unfortunate accident." Surprised, Hadwin now realized the real issue for Abigail. Control. She needed to control people so they would love her. She must have never felt anything but conditional love, and now she had conditions for everyone in her life. Immediately, Hadwin worked out an angle of escape that did not involve his family.

CHAPTER 42

Ezekiel went home. He mulled in his mind the day's events. Yeshua angry? It didn't make sense. *I have never seen Yeshua angry like that,* he thought. Rina was away, which made his life easier for the moment. Ezekiel looked for Elyam. He found him in the back trying to chop some wood for the fires over Passover.

"So, I see you have brought our animals."

"Yes. Yeshua destroyed the vendors in the Temple. These came from a farm outside of town."

"So, have you talked to Rina?"

"A little."

"You have to be braver than that, Ezekiel. The woman is looking for you to be a man."

"I don't think she really loves me. She was willing to marry Asher . . ."

"Are you dense? Do you not understand what happened? She did that to keep you safe. To keep her family safe. She doesn't have a selfish bone in her body, but you are making it all about you."

"Funny. That's kind of what she said."

"Then listen. Listen for once in your life. Understand she is not going to make the first move. She is waiting for you to forgive her. She is waiting for you to forgive yourself."

"Easier said than done," Ezekiel mumbled.

"Her, or yourself?"

"Both. I try to understand why my life has turned out this way. I try to believe in God, but everything in my life pulls me away from really believing. You know?"

"My dear Ezekiel. God is hope. I believe in God because the alternative seems to be too daunting. I know how God has blessed me. He has blessed you too."

"How has God blessed me?"

"He gave you a strong back and an incredible mind. He made you to do something, that much is clear. Do not close your heart to Him. He has rescued our people time and time again."

"And how do you know the Romans are not right? What if there are many gods and they are just as cruel and unjust as people?"

"Ezekiel, it is normal to question God's plan. But please, I beg you. Do not dishonor God or his workers. It is God who has blessed our family. Even you."

Ezekiel did not feel blessed. In fact, he felt cheated. He felt cheated from all the hard work it took to win Rina, only to have felt her rejection. He felt cheated by living for one set of values only to have people look down their noses at him for being the son of a known thief. He felt cheated because he had to take care of his mother, because his father left them at an early age to fight his war on the Romans. He also felt something else. Guilt. He left Hadwin to live the life of a slave.

He disowned his father to save his and his mother's life. He felt guilty because he entertained the thought of killing Asher. And now all of it was boiling like a cauldron in his heart.

"I don't feel blessed," said Ezekiel.

"Well, we put too much emphasis on our feelings," said Elyam.

"When you started your fishing business, did you feel like going out on the water every morning?"

"No, I didn't."

"Then why did you go out every morning?"

"Because if I didn't our family would not have food."

"Right. You knew that the work was worth it even though you felt otherwise. Rina is special . . . Why are you giving up on her again?" said Elyam.

"I don't know. I am just not in that place right now."

"Well, you know where the place is. Walk over and get in it. She is the best thing that could ever happen to you."

"Why do you keep trying to put us together? Why does it matter to you?"

"Because I have not seen my grandson happy since you have been here. Ezekiel, you act as if you do not love her but everything you do speaks of a man who is in love. I will say it again. You cannot do better than Rina."

"And what if I'm not the problem. What if it is her? Did you ever think of that?"

"It's not her, Ezekiel. You know I would do anything for you. But you have your father's stubbornness. She loves you. You just have to figure out how to speak her language."

Ezekiel felt compelled to tell Elyam the whole story. It almost slipped out. But he held his tongue. *Elyam does not need to know that Hadwin is alive and that he is in servitude to Abigail,* he thought.

The rest of the day slipped by without incident. Remembering the nuances of his lies left Ezekiel exhausted. Why did Abigail spare his life and give him the dagger? It did not make sense. This was the woman bent on killing Hadwin and avenging her brother. It would have been her right to kill them both when they attempted the ambush. They had two days until the Passover meal. The prep was done; the only things left were for Elyam to take two of the lambs to the Temple to sacrifice for the families, and they would search the household ceremonially to make sure there was no leavening agent in the house. Until then, it was life as usual.

Ezekiel sat on a bench letting his mind roam to the possibilities that Elyam was right. He had let fear keep him from the woman he wanted for life. He was closed off. The worst part of it was that he didn't know how to open up again. It was not like he didn't have money. He did. He was wanting to invest it in lands and maybe a vineyard or three. He didn't want to go back to fishing. He was tired of his fortune being made on the winds and the tides instead of steady work. Now he feared he was becoming lazy. He decided, once Passover week was done, he would find a merchant or carpenter to work for. The carpenters in Jerusalem worked with wood and stone. He could learn something, and it would keep him busy.

"Do you need to be alone, or could you use some company?" said Rina. Ezekiel hadn't noticed she was back, and the sound of her voice took him by surprise.

"Have a seat," said Ezekiel.

"It seems we've been arguing every time we see each other lately."

Ezekiel paused for a moment. "I haven't been fair to you. It's just that my whole life has been a battle. I felt as though you were too."

"Ezekiel, you're my best friend. I care about you more than anyone in the world. I just hate to think that we can't get past this."

"Yeah, I know I've been pretty foolish. Take it slow?" Ezekiel offered.

"Sure, but not too slow. You're getting pretty old," said Rina with a twinkle in her eye.

"I never thought I would see your eyes smile like that again," said Ezekiel.

Embarrassed, Rina said nothing but just inched a little closer to Ezekiel and lay her head on his shoulder. It sent a shiver up Ezekiel's spine. For once, he felt like he was home. Elyam was right. She was perfect.

Just then Ezekiel heard a noise.

"Did you hear that?" he asked Rina.

"Yes, I heard it too. It's coming from just inside that window over there," she whispered.

"Wait here," said Ezekiel. He rose from the bench and tiptoed over to the window opening. Looking down he saw a jar of water that was used to store water from the well. Taking a handful, he threw it just inside the window and heard a squeal.

"Yes, yes, I know it's wrong to eavesdrop, but I've been waiting a long time for you two to patch things up," said Bathshua.

"We are just talking," said Rina.

"Well, as long as you're just talking about marriage and then great-grandchildren. I would like to get to know them before I die." Bathshua made her way to the front door. "You kids don't know how easy you have it."

Ezekiel and Rina looked at each other and smiled. They talked for a while, catching up on the events and tragedies of the time lost between them. It felt good to reconnect. Ezekiel had wondered if he would ever reconnect with Rina or even be allowed to talk to her again. He didn't realize how much he had missed her. This was going to be the best Passover yet.

CHAPTER 43

Dismas was gaunt in demeanor. Time had lost meaning in the dungeon. The shackles rubbed his wrists and ankles raw as he sat in the corner of his cell. He heard the guards throw another prisoner in with him during the night, but he said nothing to the man who now shared the small world of darkness. Several times the man reached out, and Dismas ignored each one of his pleas.

"Do you have a name?" the man asked. "Mine is Sittish." Hour after hour the man asked his name. Still, he did not give in.

Dismas could not believe his ears. Didn't this guy take a hint? Finally worn down from the question, Dismas offered a terse response.

"With the things I have done, I don't deserve a name."

"Well, I hold true to mine. It is my family's honor."

"I suppose you hold true to your innocence as well."

"Of course. Everyone in prison is innocent," said Sittish.

Dismas forced a laugh.

"Well, we are going to die soon. Your honor will die with you as well."

"How do you know that?" asked Sittish.

"They're giving us good food. They want us to improve our strength. My guess is they want us for a show."

"A show?"

"Yes, they must want to torture us for their entertainment. The Romans are known for such things."

Dismas could see the despair on Sittish's face even through the gloom of the cell. It was not long before he could hear Sittish sobbing.

"I only came to this place to hear Yeshua and his talk of peace. I stole only what I needed to live when my men abandoned me. Surely I don't deserve to die."

"It doesn't matter what you deserve. It matters what is going to happen."

CHAPTER 44

The time for the Passover meal was upon them. Elyam reclined at the head of the table, and next to him reclined Ezekiel and then Bathshua, Aaliyah, Ester, and Rina. Each ceremoniously washed their hands in a basin provided at the entrance of the home. Since no one came from far away, they dispensed with the foot-washing ritual. The table was barely four inches from the ground. Each person reclined on their side as they ate.

Before Elyam were four cups. Each was to be ceremonially poured at the right time, and each person was to drink from them.

Elyam began with the kiddush, or prayer of sanctification.

"Blessed are you, O Lord our God, King of the universe, who has created the fruit of the vine . . . And you, O Lord our God, have given us festival days for joy, this feast of the unleavened bread, the time of our deliverance in remembrance of the departure from Egypt."

Elyam poured the first cup of wine. He then cited Exodus 6:6-7, saying, "I am the Lord, and I will bring you out from under the yoke of the Egyptians . . ." He then passed around the first cup.

Elyam pulled out the karpas, or bitter herbs. He dipped them twice, prompting the ceremonial questions from Ezekiel, the only son at the table.

"Why is this night different from all other nights? On all other nights we eat leavened or unleavened bread, but this night only unleavened bread.

"On all other nights we eat all kinds of herbs, but this night only bitter herbs. Why do we dip the herbs twice?

"On all other nights we eat meat roasted, stewed, or boiled, but on this night why only roasted meat?"

While he asked these questions Aaliyah and Ester removed all food from the table as required. The second cup was poured.

Elyam answered the questions by saying, "The father of the children of Israel was obedient to God as was his line to the line of Moses. When the children of Israel were asked to leave, they would paint their doorpost with the blood of a lamb, and they roasted that lamb. They had no time to allow their bread to rise, so we eat unleavened bread."

Elyam then began to sing. "Praise the Lord. Praise, you servants of the Lord, praise the name of the Lord. May the Lord's name be praised now and forevermore. From east to west the Lord's name is deserving of praise. The Lord is exalted over all the nations; his splendor reaches beyond the sky. Who can compare to the Lord our God, who sits on a high throne?"

While Elyam was singing, Rina smiled at Ezekiel. It was as if nothing had ever happened between the two. Ezekiel's heart jumped inside of his chest. How can I still have feelings for her? he thought. It was in that moment, that perfect moment, that Rina suddenly became more beautiful than Ezekiel had ever imagined.

Ester shot her daughter a look as if to say not now! With that look the moment was gone.

"The mountains skipped like rams, the hills like lambs. Why do you flee, O sea? Why do you turn back, O Jordan River? Why do you skip like rams, O mountains, like lambs, O hills? Tremble, O earth, before the Lord—before the God of Jacob, who turned a rock into a pool of water, a hard rock into springs of water."

Elyam prayed over the second cup. "Blessed are you, O Lord our God, King of the universe, who has created the fruit of the vine . . ." He then passed the cup.

He recited Exodus 6:6 by saying, "I will deliver you from their bondage . . ." Praying over the bread he broke it, prompting each to break their neighbor's bread one by one. Each at the table ceremoniously washed their hands again. Dipping the bread in the bitter herbs, each began to eat.

The anticipation of the meal was almost more than Ezekiel could stand. The roast lamb smelled amazing, and after the bitter herbs it tasted amazing as well. Each person was free to talk during this time as they ate. He looked once again at Rina, causing her to blush.

When they were finished, Elyam rose from his reclining position again. He poured the third cup, praying, "Blessed are you, O Lord our God, King of the universe, who brings forth bread from the earth. Blessed are you, O Lord our God, King of the universe, who has sanctified us with your commandments, and commanded us to eat unleavened bread."

Ezekiel could hardly contain his enthusiasm. He longed to be right with Rina. He longed for celebration of her as his wife. He tried to push any thought of her betrayal from his mind. His daydreaming was interrupted by the responsive prayer he was supposed to recite along with everyone else.

"The name of the Lord be blessed from now until eternity. Let us bless him of whose gifts we have partaken: Blessed be our God of whose gifts we have partaken, and by whose goodness we exist."

"Blessed are you, O Lord our God, King of the universe, who has created the fruit of the vine . . ."

Elyam, then recited from Exodus 6:6, "I will redeem you with an outstretched arm and with great judgments."

They passed around the third cup of wine, and each drank from it.

Elyam poured the fourth cup, and this time they blessed it in unison, saying, "Blessed are you, O Lord our God, King of the universe, who has created the fruit of the vine . . ."

Then Elyam recited the end of Exodus 6:6 and beginning of 7, saying, "Then I will take you as my people, and I will be your God; and you shall know that I am the Lord your God, who brought you out from under the burdens of the Egyptians."

Finally, they all sang Psalm 115 to 118.

―――――――

When everything was finished, Elyam took the lambs to the Temple. Ezekiel walked over to where Rina was still reclining.

"Would you like to go for a walk?" he asked.

"I don't know. I think Bathshua needs some help with cleaning up."

"I have more help than I need," Bathshua called from the other room. "You go and have your fun. Just not too much fun."

"C'mon. I saw a great garden near the Temple. There won't be many people around this time of night."

"Alright. Just for a little bit," said Rina. She rose slowly and yawned. "Too much wine," she said.

Ezekiel smiled. The couple picked up two oil lamps and left without another word.

The time was now considered morning as days were counted from sundown to sundown. The walk to the garden was unusually quiet. Some families were still finishing up their Passover meal, and many had just gone to sleep afterwards. Ezekiel and Rina tried to be quiet and respectful.

When they arrived in the garden the dim light of their oil lanterns cascaded off the olive trees. Ezekiel could see others who had the same idea. Lovers who wanted to walk off the wine and food they had just consumed and a few travelers who decided to camp in the garden because there were no vacancies in the inns. As they walked, they could see the oil lamps of men praying, some of whom seemed to be asleep.

A familiar voice split the night. "You can sleep later! The hour has come upon us. The Son of Man is betrayed!" It was Yeshua. Ezekiel heard the moan of what appeared to be Simon and several others. The commotion was so out of place that neither Rina nor Ezekiel saw the Roman soldiers arriving with Judas. The crowd closed around them. Ezekiel pulled Rina to hide behind a stout olive tree. Ezekiel decided to climb up and get a better look.

"What do you see from up there?"

"SHHH! I'll tell you when I get down," said Ezekiel. From his perch he could see a man greeting Yeshua with a kiss on each cheek. In an instant, the Roman guards seized Yeshua, prompting Simon to pull out his sword and swing for one of the soldier's head. The soldier ducked his head to the side, but not enough. The sword sliced off his ear.

"If you live by the sword you will die by it. Put it away. If I wanted, I could have a whole host of angels protect me. But it must be this way," said Yeshua. The moment caught all by surprise, allowing Yeshua to pick up the ear and place it back on the soldier's head. The Roman soldiers then led him away.

"They are arresting him," said Ezekiel. "I wonder if they're taking him to the same place my father is held."

"Ezekiel, you can't be serious. They are going to kill him. And you if you go after him."

"I have to try to get to him. Are you coming with me?" Ezekiel dropped to the ground beneath the olive tree.

"No!" Rina backed away. "I didn't agree to this. You cannot do this now."

"I have to. I have to get a message to my father."

"What . . . what if you get killed? What will I do then? What will your poor mother or your grandparents do then?"

"I can't explain it, but I have to get to him," Ezekiel said. He had kept the dagger strapped to his thigh under his garments since he received it from Abigail. *If I can return the dagger, then maybe my father will be released.* He hated the thought of leaving Rina there alone, but he had to.

"Listen, there's not much time. Take the lanterns and go straight back to the house. Try to stay close to other family groups for safety. I'll see you soon."

He didn't want to put her in further danger. Walking fast, he walked to catch up with the soldiers, who were now a good way off in the distance. He then broke into a run to see where Yeshua would be held for his trial.

CHAPTER 45

R ina ran all the way back to their house. She didn't stop until she saw Elyam walking back from the Temple.

"Slow down there, child!" she heard him say.

"Grandfather, Ezekiel has gone to chase after Yeshua. He has been arrested, and Ezekiel thinks he can get a message to his father!"

"What? You're kidding! Here is what I want you to do. I want you to get Aaliyah and your mom. I will retrace the steps to the Roman court. The prison is not far from there. I will bring Ezekiel back. Let's meet in front of the Temple at the south gate. You got it?" said Elyam.

"Yes, I got it," said Rina.

"He is going to be alright. Believe that!" said Elyam. He turned and walked as fast as his old legs would take him.

CHAPTER 46

E zekiel was gaining ground on the group of soldiers. The rest of the group had dispersed. Simon was the only one who was even close. Ezekiel caught up to him.

"I don't know you," said Simon.

"Don't be silly. We worked together in Tiberias."

"Yes, but people don't know that. I don't want to be seen with anyone who's a part of this."

"Alright. I'll just be on my way," said Ezekiel. Looking to his right, he could see that the prison was next to the court, where two Roman guards stood at the front ironclad door. Ezekiel walked up to one guard. "Sir, is there a man named Dismas being held here?"

The guards said nothing. They just stared straight ahead as if he were not there.

"Excuse me, I'm trying to see if there is a man . . ."

"I heard you. Now get lost. Prisoners of Rome have no name. These men will be executed at dawn."

"Well, you see, that is why I came. If I can buy his freedom . . ."

Ezekiel was interrupted by the men's laughter.

"You can't buy his freedom, boy. He is marked for death."

"If you will just give me a chance to explain . . ."

One of the guards broke ranks and pushed Ezekiel out into the street. Drawing his sword, he hit him with the pummel and swung his sword back and forth. Ezekiel fell backwards to the ground. A crowd formed around the scene, people coming out from all over. Ezekiel tried to get up, and again he was struck by the flat part of the Roman gladius. He thought of pulling the dagger, but he knew at this point it would mean certain death. The soldier sheathed his sword and delivered punishing blows to Ezekiel's face to the point where he fell onto his back once again. The Roman drew his sword and held it high with both hands, about to plunge it into Ezekiel's abdomen.

"Wait!" said a voice in a Samaritan accent. Ezekiel could not make out who it was.

"Let me kill him. I am owed retribution from this snake."

The Roman guard glanced at where the voice came from. "And why should I let you kill this man?"

"Because he gave me this." The Samaritan pulled out his right stump where a hand should have been. Then Ezekiel recognized him. He was the netmaker.

The other guard called, "We don't have time for this foolishness!"

"I take it you have a sword?" the Roman asked.

The Samaritan pulled it out from under his tunic. "Yes, I do," he said. He spat on the ground next to Ezekiel's face.

"Then he is all yours." The Roman turned to leave.

The Samaritan turned to Ezekiel and grabbed him by the back of the cloak while still clutching his blade in the same hand. "When I tell you to scream, you let out a scream like your life depended on it," he whispered.

Dragging him to an alleyway, he whispered, "Now!" Ezekiel screamed as if he had been stabbed. "Good, that's enough."

"Why are you helping me?"

"I recognized you as a Galilean. I couldn't believe this was the same boy who turned me down because of my heritage. I thought to myself 'I could let him die' or 'I could save his life and have someone who will buy all their nets from me.'" The Samaritan smiled. Ezekiel tried to stand up and staggered.

"Whoa, whoa, easy now. You took quite a beating," said the Samaritan. Ezekiel started to laugh through his agony.

"What's so funny?"

"I . . . am out . . . of the . . . fishing . . . business." This brought a smile to the Samaritan's face.

"Then you will be in my debt forever then." And he turned and walked away. Ezekiel tried to stand once more. Once he was able to get his feet under him, he limped back toward the street. Blood was dripping from his nose. He reached up and felt a trickle from his right ear as well.

As the shock wore off, his head became a weight that was difficult to hold up. Pain shot through his whole body, and he fell to the ground. He tried to pick himself back up, but he just fell back down again. Every muscle in his body tensed as he tried to get his bearings. He still had the dagger strapped to his side. He didn't even have the chance to make the trade. One more try to get up. Wincing in pain, he willed himself to his feet. Putting one foot in front of the other, he began to get his stride once again.

"Ezekiel!" shouted Elyam. Ezekiel could see a blurry shape rushing to his side.

"Ezekiel, my boy, what happened?"

"I won the fight!"

"I'd hate to see what happens when you lose. Come on!" Elyam put Ezekiel's arm over his shoulder. They limped toward the path leading to their house. On the way Ezekiel could see three figures coming toward them. It was Rina, Aaliyah, and Ester.

"Thank God you found him," said Aaliyah.

"I told you . . . you were going to get yourself killed!" said Rina. Ester said nothing.

"Bathshua is at home. She needs to rest after making the Passover meal," Aaliyah said.

"So, let's get Ezekiel home then."

"NO!" said Ezekiel. "I need to see what happens! Just give me some of your wine and I will be alright." Elyam handed him his wineskin, and Ezekiel drank from it hungrily.

CHAPTER 47

The trial of Yeshua was a mockery even by Roman standards. Pilate heard the case himself and, ever the politician, decided to go with a lesser punishment to appease the crowd. Having Yeshua whipped with the nine-tailed whip was punishment that many people did not live through. Since his wife, Procla, had a dream about this man, Pilate did not want to be the one to put a holy man to death. He himself could find no fault in him. He also knew he could lose control of the crowd—something that would relieve him of his position if he presided over an uprising. Two thieves and a murderer named Barabbas were scheduled to be crucified this weekend already. That might keep the crowd's bloodlust to a minimum. The high priest Caiaphas was popular among the Jews, and he could quell this potential uprising, but he seemed to push for the execution of Yeshua more than the others. Pilate awaited word that the sentence was carried out, ordering a basin of water to rid himself ceremonially when the time was right.

"Prepare Barabbas to go before the crowd," he instructed his chief officer. "When this Yeshua is back from his beating, we will appeal to the kind nature of the people to contrast him with a murderer."

"Yes, my lord," said the centurion. Pilate eased back into his chair. His head splitting with stress, he took a swig from his wine cup and prayed to the gods that he was not in the wrong here.

The beating took less than an hour. His personal guard carried it out. The man they now brought before him was almost unrecognizable. The look of agony on Yeshua's face perplexed Pilate. This was by far the hardest thing he'd ever had to do. Every other man he sent to the cross deserved the punishment, either through sedition, murder, or larceny. This man was none of those things. His claims pertained to the spiritual realm, not the physical. His authority was not about overthrowing the Roman government. There was nothing to be made here that even came close to that. This man was urging peace, forgiveness, and love. Surely these were not the enemy of Rome. The man who now stood before him did not deserve to die.

Rising from his chair, Pilate walked to the veranda where a crowd had gathered outside. The crowd was chanting, "Crucify him! Crucify him!" Raising both hands in the air, Pilate was nearly successful in calming the crowd and said, "I come to you with a choice. I can find no fault in this man. We have already scourged him. Is that not enough?"

"Crucify him! Crucify him!" the crowd chanted.

"It is customary to release one prisoner at the end of Passover. I have on my right Barabbas. He is a murderer who has a long list of crimes against Rome and the Jews. Surely you would want me to release Yeshua as opposed to this man?" said Pilate.

"Give us Barabbas! Crucify Yeshua!" a man in the crowd said. Everyone chanted, "Release Barabbas! Crucify Yeshua!" Pilate's heart sank. This was the last hope for this man. Turning to one of his servants, he said, "Bring out the water basin."

Immediately it was brought to him and set on the ledge. He dipped his hands in the water.

"I wash my hands of him," Pilate said. "My centurions will carry out your punishment under your law only. Not Rome's." The guards seized Yeshua and handed him over to the crowds, who put a purple robe on him and placed a crown of thorns on his brow.

Pilate retreated to his inner chamber. "May the gods choose mercy when they see the untenable situation I was in," he said aloud.

Rina could tell Ezekiel was regaining a lot of his strength. He still could not keep up with the rest of his family. Elyam agreed to go slower with him, and they lagged behind. When they reached the crowd, Yeshua had already been given over to the will of the people, and they could see the purple robe and the crown of thorns. Rina pushed her way to the front of the crowd. She wanted to know what was going to happen. Roman centurions seemed to appear out of nowhere. Two more men were in chains with them. Rina's heart sank. One of them was Dismas. She had not seen him since she was a little girl, but she was sure of it.

She had seen a crucifixion only once before, and that was way off in the distance. She couldn't stay and she couldn't leave either. Each man was made to carry his own cross, the soldiers cracking whips to keep them motivated. Yeshua was so covered in blood he was almost unrecognizable. The group began to move, the crowd jeering and following in lock step. Rina could not believe how many children were there with their parents. Surely these people had enough sense to keep their kids away from this kind of violence. She grew up in an environment where her father did his best to keep her away from these kinds of things.

She did not join in the chanting. She just kept her head down. In the commotion, her mother and Aaliyah must have been pushed back by the crowd. She couldn't worry about that now. The walk to Golgotha was longer than she expected. Fighting back tears, she didn't want the other people to think she felt in any way sorry for them. They were so mean. Every time she was about to collect her thoughts, another crack of the whip came. It made her jump every time. Each time she heard a scream in pain, she winced. Yeshua was the first in line to carry his cross. Rina could see his body give way under its weight, and he stumbled. The centurion picked a man from the crowd to carry it.

CHAPTER 48

E zekiel and Elyam caught up to the women by this point. Ezekiel was feeling a little better. At least that is what he told himself. When the crowd spread out at Golgotha, the place of the skull, Ezekiel could see a little bit better. Still holding out hope that his father was not one of the prisoners to be executed, he sat down on a stump to take a breath.

Elyam, Ester, and Aaliyah all stopped as well. Ezekiel was glad for the rest. It was as if all his blood rushed into his head in a moment. His nose began to bleed again, and now his eye was swelling up.

All his hopes that his father was not being executed were shattered on the first strike of the hammer. The scream he heard was from Dismas, he knew it. Immediately, Ezekiel tried to get up and move toward the sound. Elyam held him back.

"Slow down, there is nothing you can do," said Elyam. Aaliyah and Ester were crying, and Ezekiel had never seen this look on his grandfather's face before. If he could cry, he would. He once held on to the dream that someday he would know his father and his father would somehow show that he cared for his family. Now, in a slow and agonizing moment, he knew his hopes of knowing his father and gaining his father's approval were dashed. He didn't want to look, but the spectacle demanded his attention. After the three men were nailed to their crosses amid the screams, he could see them being raised. Now he could see his father clearly.

To his surprise he saw Sittish on one side of Yeshua and his father on the other. He was still too far away to hear anything they said. The crowd was too thick for them to push through. So the four of them had to stay to the outer reaches of the crowd. Upon seeing his father tortured, Ezekiel sank to his knees and threw up. Moving to all fours, he heaved again and again. Aaliyah pulled his curly hair back. Elyam tried his best to keep the crowd out of the way. Ester put her hand on Aaliyah's shoulder for moral support. No one knew what to say, so they said nothing.

CHAPTER 49

Rina was close enough to hear the talking. As some of the men gambled for the crucified men's possessions, she could hear the conversations on the crosses.

"Father forgive them. They do not know what they are doing," said Yeshua in a strained voice. Rina wondered how a man who was being tortured could forgive others. She was so close she could read the sign they placed over his head. It read "This is the King of the Jews." She wanted to focus more on Dismas, but she knew Dismas deserved everything that was happening to him. But Yeshua? Yeshua preached about peace. Doing good to those who persecute you. He did not seem like the revolutionary they claimed he was. This was proving to take a long time. She wondered if the crowds would die down after a while.

She wanted to leave but was afraid she would miss something. She prayed for a miracle, and the miracle never came. Blood trickled down from Yeshua's hands. Gasping for air as he tried to put pressure on the nail in his feet, it was at that moment that she heard Sittish speak up first.

"If you are truly the Messiah, why don't you save yourself and us?"

Dismas replied, "Don't you fear God? We have both been sentenced for the things we have done. It is right that we are being punished. This man has done nothing wrong!" Turning his head toward Yeshua, he said, "Please, will you remember me when you enter into your kingdom?"

Yeshua lifted his head. "Dismas, truly you will be with me when I enter paradise."

Rina could not believe what she just heard. Dismas was forgiven his sins by the one who claimed to be the Son of God. Rina tried to push back against the crowd. She could take no more. She had to find Ezekiel and tell him. "Let me through," she said. She broke through the crowd and made her way to the back. It took her quite some time to find Ezekiel and the rest of the family.

The sun was now in the middle of the sky. As soon as she found the family the world lost the sun—as if night had fallen early.

The ground shook, sending many running for their homes. The few who remained had nowhere to go. Rina held onto Ezekiel, holding him up. Elyam held onto both Aaliyah and Ester. When the ground stopped shaking, they decided it was time to go home. The darkness had not waned, and they were standing there with no oil for their lamps.

"Ezekiel, I have something to tell you when we get home," said Rina. Her words barely registered with Ezekiel, who was now feeling the full weight of the pain from the beating he took. The grief he felt at that moment almost kept him from getting up. Everything around him was blurry. He knew he had to press on, but he couldn't. He couldn't watch the spectacle anymore. Dismas, his father, was dead or soon would be. He hated him. He hated him because of the way he left. He hated him for the time he felt was more important to fight a losing battle. He hated himself for not taking responsibility when he could have. He deserved the beating. He probably deserved worse. Ezekiel the coward. So afraid for his and his mother's life that he failed to fight the Romans off of his father. He failed to rescue him. He was so blinded by his own ambition that he didn't see the big picture, and now his father was dead. Maybe Hadwin too. If God was real, then he was cruel and didn't fully understand the weakness of men. Still, a beacon deep in his soul told him a different story. A story of redemption if he would just listen. He couldn't listen now. He just wanted to die. He turned once more to look back at his father hanging there. He heard one last scream—"It is finished!"—from Yeshua.

"He tried to tell me! He tried to tell me, and I wouldn't listen!" A rage built up inside of Ezekiel.

"You don't understand!" shouted Rina.

"No, you don't understand. He tried to tell me back when I sold the dagger! He told me someone would die if I sold it. If I didn't return the money! He didn't tell me it was my father!" Ezekiel broke down and sobbed, falling to his knees and then curling up on the ground like a baby.

"Ezekiel, I heard something. Something Yeshua said to your father. He forgave his sins!" Rina shouted over the noise of the crowd rushing past.

"He couldn't even save himself from that cross. How could he forgive my father's sins?" Ezekiel cried. He was hyperventilating so much that Elyam thought he would pass out right there. Rain had started by this time, and Elyam hurried everyone. They all did their best to lift Ezekiel, but he was having none of it. Rina elected to stay with him as the rest ran to their house.

"Just let me die," said Ezekiel.

"No!" said Rina. Ezekiel started to fade out of consciousness.

"No! You can't die on me, Ezekiel! I need you! We all need you! You can't do this!"

"Just let me die! It's my fault. All of it. Just let me die!"

"I am not going to let you die, Ezekiel! I didn't when we were kids, and I'm not now!" she cried.

With that Ezekiel felt himself going to sleep. He never intended to wake up. If his will was strong enough he would just fade into nonexistence. The whole world went black.

That was the plan, but God, or the gods, would not let him die. He woke the next morning inside his room, on his mat. He pieced together the fragments of memories after Elyam had brought his donkey. How the old man had lifted him onto it was a miracle in itself. Rina was there when he woke. It was obvious she had been crying.

He knew he was awake, but he felt as though he were dying. Rina tried to offer him some food. He didn't want it.

"Do you want to talk about it?"

"No. Leave me alone."

"Well, when you are ready, I'm here," said Rina. Elyam entered the room with a wineskin full of water. Rina stood up and walked out.

"She hasn't left your side since you collapsed out there. You can't buy that kind of love or devotion." Elyam left the wineskin on the floor next to Ezekiel. "Drink it. You may not want to live, but she needs you to."

Ezekiel still said nothing. He just pretended his family was not there. Elyam nodded his head and left the room. Walking past Rina, he said, "Just give him time. He will come around."

The next day was the same. Ezekiel did not say anything to anyone. He just moped around. Aaliyah and Rina both tried to talk to him. He would just go for a walk. Ezekiel could not help but overhear a conversation about the previous day's events. They took his father to an unmarked grave. Yeshua was the only one of the three who had a grave worthy of anyone of respect. Ezekiel could not bring himself to speak. He just went about his chores in silence.

On the third day Ezekiel went for his walk. His spirits were lifted slightly as his wounds began to heal. He still could not bring himself to talk about it to anyone, but for the first time he felt the possibility of moving on, at least for the moment. That was his plan. To just walk away. To walk away from the pain, from Rina, from his faith, and everything he knew. He decided to pack his things. Rina was better off without him. In time they would all see it. They would see the phony he was.

He gathered his things early in the morning before the sun was up and slipped out of the house. When he reached the outskirts of the city, he saw a lone figure sitting on a log. He tried to walk past without being noticed, but the man called to him in a voice he knew all too well.

"Ezekiel, why don't you come over and sit with me for a while?" Ezekiel, about to faint, did as he was told. He couldn't help but stare at the man whose death he had witnessed just three days before.

"You are here? How are you here? I saw you die."

"Death cannot hold the Son of God."

"So, if you conquered death, then why can my father not be here with you?"

"Your father could not come back from the grave. But I tell you the truth, he is in a better place than you could ever imagine," said Yeshua.

"So, you did save yourself. You just didn't see fit to save anyone else," said Ezekiel.

"Pull that dagger out," said Yeshua. Ezekiel, amazed that he knew he had it, did as he was told.

"The craftsman who made this dagger used fire to refine the gold and fire to forge this blade. Through pain and suffering, you are saved. So was your father."

"I don't understand," said Ezekiel.

"Remember when I wanted to make you a fisher of men?"

"Yes."

"Well, in a similar way, Dismas is my thief now. He is forgiven. He is in heaven."

Ezekiel felt as though someone had punched him in the stomach. It was all too much. *How could my father be in heaven?* he asked himself.

"Will I ever see him again?" he asked.

"That is up to you," said Yeshua. He rose from his seated position and Ezekiel could see the scars where the nails tore through his flesh. His forehead still bore the marks of the thorny crown. Looking up the road, Yeshua pointed.

"I believe your future is headed this way."

Ezekiel looked up and saw Rina headed toward them.

AUTHOR'S NOTE

It has been such a rewarding journey writing *Yeshua's Thief*. The best part is that the story isn't over. As Christ-followers, our stories are never over. Be on the lookout for book two, *Yeshua's Slave*. In the meantime, visit yeshuasthief.com to read blog posts, short stories, and learn more about Yeshua. Sign up for my email list and get exclusive content, including stories that tie into Yeshua's world.

I love hearing from my readers and fellow writers. Please check out my website—readdison.com—for news, blog, products, and books. I look forward to seeing what God does with your story! I can also be found on Facebook at www.facebook.com/yeshuasthief and a myriad of other social media platforms.

ABOUT THE AUTHOR

R.E. Addison is an assistant pastor in South Florida. He and his wife Blanca have two children, Ryan and Karlie. He holds a Bachelor's Degree in Philosophy and Religion from Palm Beach Atlantic University and a Master of Business Administration from Ohio Christian University. He has written many plays, including *Yeshua's Thief the Musical* and *Bamboozling Scrooge*, adapted into a book later in 2021. Also, there are plans for the subsequent novels *Yeshua's Slave* and *Yeshua's Way*.

You can find the author on social media, or look him up on his website readdison.com.

He would love to hear from you, so shoot him an email at readdison@yeshuasthief.net.

If you would like more information on who Yeshua is, please scan this QR code for a short video explaining how you can know Yeshua in a personal way.

A free ebook edition is available with the purchase of this book.

To claim your free ebook edition:

Visit MorganJamesBOGO.com
Sign your name CLEARLY in the space
Complete the form and submit a photo of
the entire copyright page
You or your friend can download the ebook
to your preferred device

Morgan James
BOGO™

A **FREE** ebook edition is available for you
or a friend with the purchase of this print book.

CLEARLY SIGN YOUR NAME ABOVE

Instructions to claim your free ebook edition:
1. Visit MorganJamesBOGO.com
2. Sign your name CLEARLY in the space above
3. Complete the form and submit a photo
   of this entire page
4. You or your friend can download the ebook
   to your preferred device

Print & Digital Together Forever.

Snap a photo

Free ebook

Read anywhere